To: Dar

Τhis 1 Ρromise

THIS I PROMISE

SHAYLYNN WILBON

authorHOUSE®

AuthorHouse™
1663 Liberty Drive
Bloomington, IN 47403
www.authorhouse.com
Phone: 1-800-839-8640

Published by AuthorHouse   11/26/2012

ISBN: 978-1-4772-9073-6 (sc)
ISBN: 978-1-4772-9074-3 (hc)
ISBN: 978-1-4772-9072-9 (e)

Library of Congress Control Number: 2012921729

DEDICATIONS

To my family.

ACKNOWLEDGMENTS

———————

A special thank you to my mom and dad for believing in my dream.
Thank you Heidi for helping me with editing.

CHAPTER 1

*a*n adventure. That's all I want. All I ask is for one adventure in my life. Most people consider getting married, having kids and then grandchildren as an adventure. Not me. The adventure I seek is one that you would hear in fairy tales and in fantasy novels. I know I can never have that sort of thing so I figure the closest I'll get to the adventure I want is to finish school, go to university and get a job that will provide lots of money. That way I can travel to exotic places and try to find what I'm looking for, or at least something close.

I want out of this place, this house, not because of my parents—I love my parents very much—but because I need an adventure. Everyday life seems pointless, so boring and so repetitive in my opinion. Every day goes by pretty much the same. Monday to Friday, wake up at seven, prepare for school till eight, take the bus to school and get to class by eight thirty. Make it through my boring morning classes, eat lunch with my best friends, make it through my boring afternoon classes, get home at four, finish homework, read or do whatever else I feel like doing, get ready for bed, go to sleep at ten and then day after day. On the weekends I do other, more interesting things, but for the most part, my days are pretty much the same and by that I mean—uneventful.

Even I haven't really changed. For most of my life, my hair has been long, wavy and dark brown, and always worn down. My eyes a nice, deep chocolate brown, portraying the same, expression of longing, and for as long as I can remember, my body has been long and thin, with my skin having been a never-changing tan colour. I basically look like a younger version of my mother, except she has blonde hair; I get my brown hair from my father.

I've been living in this house for all of my 18 years, and the only place I have not memorized—or even seen!—is the third floor. My parents have forbidden me to go up there, and until recently I've never felt much interest, anyway. I always just assumed that it was like the rest of the house: boring and old, with its plain walls, wooden floors and antique furniture. But for some reason today, I'm very curious and wondering . . . What is up there? Maybe my curiosity is due to the boredom of having the same surroundings all my life. And since my parents are out visiting friends, now would be the perfect time to explore beyond the staircase.

I have an uneasy feeling as I ascend the stairs. I don't know why—how bad could whatever is up there possibly be? I turn the corner and realize that at the top of the stairway, there is only one door. I hope it isn't locked. I start to reach for the door handle and then slowly turn it, taking a deep breath. The room is empty, except for one dresser.

It's a simple, small dresser. Very old-fashioned. It matches the rest of the house. It's made out of solid oak, smooth and shiny, and for some unknown reason I feel drawn to it. Maybe it's because of the beautiful, intricate designs on the front that look like they were carved by hand.

I'm kind of disappointed. I figured there would be something more exciting in this hidden room especially since Mom and Dad forbid me to come in here. But, in a way, I'm not at all surprised—nothing in this house has ever been exciting.

I almost turn back to leave the forbidden room when the thought crosses me mind: *What's in the dresser?* I walk up to it and pull the door open slowly, but just like the room, the dresser is empty. Out of sheer frustration, I shove the dresser to the side. But, wait. Behind it I see a large, thick, seemingly metal door.

Suddenly the feeling of uneasiness returns. But I can't stop now or I won't be able to stop wondering what lies waiting behind the door. I move the dresser completely out of the way and grab the handle of the hidden door, turning it in great anticipation.

Oh no! It's locked! Just my luck, now I really won't be able to sleep.

I put the dresser back in place, descend the stairs and go to my room, which has a little bit more life than the rest of the house because it's more colourful. It's small, but I don't mind. It has a double bed with a brown headboard. The bedspread is white with giant pink roses on it. When my parents saw it at the store, they thought it was just so clever to get it for me because my name is Rosalie and my nickname is Rose. They always buy me things with roses on them. Sometimes they even buy me the flower because they saw them at the store and they were reminded of me.

I also have a dark brown wooden dresser that matches my head board and a closet full of clothes. I have a laptop and a stereo system, but my favourite part about my room is the art—my art. I like to think of myself as an artist because I create art and I love to draw. I don't particularly like to draw for other people because what they want never reflects what I feel inside. I like to draw when I feel like it, and I prefer to draw what I feel.

On my walls hang my paintings and drawings, none of them framed. I mostly draw people because I find it is easier to portray feelings and thoughts through their facial expressions. The people I draw usually portray deep and intense feelings like sadness, anger or love.

Sometimes I find myself in a bit of a dilemma. Sometimes when I sit down in front of a blank canvas with a pencil in my hand, I cannot think of what to draw. I feel bored, the same way I usually feel. I've drawn someone with that expression so many times, and it's getting old. *What else do I feel?* I ask myself. The answer is nothing, really. I am not angry, I'm not sad and I'm not really happy either. I sigh, put my pencil down, grab a book from my bedside table and decide to lie down to read.

I'm unable to stop thinking about that annoying door, so I decide to go for a walk. Maybe I'll even be able to come up with something to draw.

I head downstairs to the main floor and go outside. It is nice outside. The sun is shining, and there is barely a cloud in the sky. The warmth of the sun feels nice on my face. I take a deep breath and smell the fresh air, clearing my head. Next I listen to the sounds of the forest by our house. It is quiet, the rustling of the leaves of the trees, the only sound. I then decide to wander through the forest.

I walk down our driveway and into the forest. There is a narrow path that leads to a fallen tree; I made this path. After years of walking through this forest, I know it like the back of my hand, but my favourite spot has always been by the fallen tree. Sometimes I bring out a pad of paper and a pencil, sit down on the tree trunk and draw what I see.

I arrive at the tree and sit down. Then I lean my head back, close my eyes and daydream. I imagine myself on an adventure, putting myself in the place of one of the many characters I've read about. I sit there for a long time before finally heading back to my house. Once there, I opt to watch TV until I go to bed.

The next day, my alarm clock wakes me up. I get up and get ready for school. When I'm ready, I head outside to the bus stop and wait for my bus. As I am waiting, my hand automatically touches the necklace I always wear around my neck. The necklace has a little red rose being held in place by a thin, silver chain. I don't simply wear it because it is pretty, which it is, but I also wear it because my parents insist that I do. I'm not sure why, but every time I ask they simply say, "Because it looks nice on you." Then they change the subject and I let them because it's not that big of a deal as to why they want me to wear it. It's not like I mind wearing it all of the time.

When the bus arrives, I hop on, pay the bus driver and sit down. When I arrive at school, I get off of the bus and go to class. During class, my mind wanders. I didn't get much sleep last night—I was too busy thinking about what could be behind that mystery door. It was as if it was calling to me all night. Even now, I find myself thinking of different things that could be hidden in there. Money? Jewels? A dead body? I hold in a laugh at that last one, which is ridiculous and highly unlikely.

At lunch, I grab the lunch I packed for myself and go sit at one of the tables outside to eat. A few moments later, Adam and Macy come and join me. Macy is very tiny; she is much shorter than me, and she's thin. She has the most beautiful blonde curls and blue eyes, and she is so sweet, though she is very shy and quiet around people other than me and Adam. She reminds me of a little fairy. I once drew her in the form of a fairy, and she really liked the picture.

Adam is tall and has short brown hair and stunning green eyes. I once drew him in black and white; his green eyes were the only colour on the picture which made them stand out like they do in real life. He has an athletic build, but he doesn't play any sports and prefers academics.

Our conversations usually consist of my art, Adam's academic stuff and Macy's style tips (she loves fashion and that kind of thing. She's always trying to dress Adam and I.), or a bit of all three. Today I am more quiet than usual because my mind is elsewhere. Adam and Macy don't seem to notice, though.

When lunch is over, I go to my afternoon classes, where I continue to think about what could be behind that door. When the final bell rings, everyone rushes to go home.

I arrive home, throw my bag in my room and find myself going back to the third floor. After going through the first door and moving the dresser again. I stare at the door and it looks back, mocking me. I stand there for a while, thinking of how I might open it without my parents knowing. I'm not worried about them finding me here—they are still at work.

As I am about to leave, I realize maybe the key to the door is in the dresser. After all, the space is big, and I didn't look too closely. I could have easily missed a small key. With new hope inside me, I turn back to the dresser. I open it again, and this time I look more carefully. Still nothing, but it's dark. With some hope, I run my hands along the edges. All of a sudden I feel something! I grab it eagerly, and sure enough, it's a small key that easily fits into the palm of my hand. It seems to be made out of brass, and it looks very old. No surprise there.

I move the dresser out of the way and approach the door once again, my heart pounding with excitement. I put the key into the key hole, and luckily it slides in perfectly. I turn it and hear the little click that signifies that the door has been unlocked.

I reach for the handle, turn it and slowly open the door. Wider, wider—but suddenly the door bursts open with a flash of light that's so blinding that I have to close my eyes. After about five seconds, the light dimmed enough for me to sneak a look.

From the door emerges a god-like figure, tall and imposing. I'm trapped in a state between disbelief, shock and fear. I am frozen in place, only able to stare in awe. It looks like flames are surrounding the figure, which I'm fairly certain is male. He takes one step towards me, forcing me to take one step back.

The blinding light dims even more, and I can now make out his features. He looks terrifying and beautiful at the same time. He seems to be about my age, maybe a year or two older at most. His eyes are pure black and filled with a look of hatred that makes me take another step back in terror. The features on his face are sharp and fierce: High cheekbones lead to a square jaw set in a straight line. His lips look soft and full, contrasting with the rest of his face and the expression they hold, which is one of distaste.

As I look at his face, I can tell he is scrutinizing me as I was him. Not wanting to meet his eyes, I examine the rest of him, noting the way his shoulders are squared and his body is lean yet muscular. If this man hadn't just stepped out of the door with piercing black eyes, I might find him attractive. In a way I still do, but it's overcome by the fear.

As I bring my eyes back up to his face, I see that a new look has come over his features: determination. Before I can register what is happening, he is closing in on me.

I feel relief as I hear my parents' car pulling into the driveway, the only sound that can get through to me in this moment. Unable to scream, I turn and run for the door. All of a sudden the brightness intensifies, and I see a ball of light fly past me, missing me by mere inches. When it goes through the wall, I realize the ball was not of light but of fire. I start screaming as more of them shoot past me.

I run down the stairs, four at a time, nearly tripping with each step. Until of course, on the last step, I do. Figures.

I lie on the ground and turn my head to see how close he is. He is halfway down the stairs. I think, *This is it. I may die here and now.* I see his hands beginning to glow as he forms another ball of fire. Just as he is about to throw it at me, the door opens and a fireball is now flying towards *him*. It hits him, and he falls to the ground from the impact.

I feel my parents' hands grabbing me and pulling me to the door roughly, but at the moment it's the most comforting touch in the world. The next thing I know is that we're in the car driving well over the speed limit away from the old (and once) boring house. Suddenly I miss its boringness, and I wonder, *What the hell just happened?*

CHAPTER 2

$\mathcal{I}$ decide to voice my thoughts and question my parents, "What the hell was that?"

My dad starts explaining in a reluctant voice. "There are some . . . people who can wield fire. We are called Fire Populous. There are some Fire Populous' who have bad intentions, just like with humans. You can probably guess that those of us with good intentions must keep the bad ones under control; we call them the Fire Demons. That's what attacked you back there. The Fire Demons were starting to get a bit out of hand, so to get them back under control, the Fire Populous had to lock up one of the . . ." He hesitates, considering his words. "One of the more powerful ones."

"*What?*" is all I could manage to choke out. I start to babble uncontrollably. "What are you talking about? Wait, is this some kind of joke? 'Cause it's not funny . . . Wait, what about the other elements? Am I one of these fire wielders, or whatever? When is the hidden camera going to pop out, and I'm going to discover I'm on *Prank Patrol?*"

My mother steps in this time. "It's the same with the other elements, but because ours is fire, we tend to get a little touchier. Even the good can sometimes get out of hand, which makes you wonder just how bad the bad ones are. And yes, you are one of the Fire Populous, but you have not been properly trained, so you will not be able to use your powers yet."

"This can't be happening!" I shout. "If you're trying to prank me, it should be at least somewhat believable! This kind of stuff just doesn't happen. And by the way, where are we going?"

"We're going to a place where he can't get to you."

"If I need to be in a place where he can't get to me, then why was he locked up in our house in the first place?" I ask.

"None of that matters now. All that matters is getting you to safety."

We drive for what feels like hours, passing nothing but trees. Finally, I begin to see water; we drive a little more and stop at a dock. We get out, and by the dock I see a boat.

"Get in," my father orders.

"Not until you tell me where we're going!" I say, feeling a bit off-guard and thus standing my ground.

My mother cuts in just before my father can say anything. "We will explain things to you in the boat. Get in."

I glare at them and reluctantly get in the boat, figuring it's my best chance to finally get some straight answers to what is happening to me.

My parents follow behind me and we all sit down. My father starts the boat. The motor groans and then suddenly starts, and before I know what is happening, we're speeding across the water.

"Okay, explain," I demand. "You promised."

My mother takes a deep breath. "We're going to an island. The island is the safest place for us to be right now, because the other Fire Populous will protect us."

"How many are there?"

"On the island, there is a whole kingdom full of them. There may be others we are unaware of elsewhere, but that is quite rare. They have been around for many centuries protecting the world from the Fire Demons."

"I see. You really expect me to believe this?" I ask.

"We will prove it to you once we get to safety," my father says.

"If I'm really a Fire Populous, then why am I just finding out about this?" I ask.

"Because we thought it would be safer for you," Mother explains.

"Safer?" I ask.

"We believed that if you didn't know you were a Fire Populous, then you would be safe from the Fire Demons."

"Yet you had one locked in a room in our house?!" I say.

My Father cuts in. "If you had listened to us and you hadn't been snooping around, this would never have happened!"

"Well, sorry for snooping around in my own house! Besides, you never actually told me why I wasn't allowed up there!" I yell.

"We thought that simply telling you would be enough, since you never questioned us about it before!" My father exclaims.

"Stop fighting!" my Mother interjects. That immediately shuts us both up.

We go the rest of the way in silence, and it takes roughly 20 minutes. When we finally get there, my father stops the boat and we get out. I notice that my parents are careful not to touch the water. It's something that I've been noticing more and more. They never take showers, or wash their hands or even drink water. Could this have something to do with the whole Fire Populous thing? All of a sudden, it hits me. "Is this why you always make me wear this necklace? Does it protect me from the water?" I ask.

"Yes," Mother says. "Without that necklace, water hurts a lot and can kill you if you're in it for too long."

"Why don't you guys have necklaces to protect you from the water?"

"Because that necklace was made a long time ago, by a Water Populous but that Water Populous only made one. Fire Populous have tried to make more, but have not succeeded. You have the only one in existence."

I look over at the island where we have just arrived. It is beautiful and majestic, full of trees and life. There is green all around me, and sand beneath my feet. My parents start walking, and I figure there's nothing else to do but follow.

They lead me into a dense jungle. As we walk, I ask, "So do the Fire Populous just wield fire, or do they do something else?"

"We only wield fire, but by wielding fire, we make it possible for humans to build fire. We are basically the personification of fire. Without fire, we do not exist, without us, fire does not exist. It's the same for the other elements as well," Mother says.

Although there is no path, they seem to know exactly where they're going. As we walk, all I can see is trees—trees with flowers, trees with vines, trees with birds. Then my parents stop. I look up and see a little village. Weird—you wouldn't expect to see one in the middle of the jungle.

The houses are all lined up on both sides of a little gravel road. The road goes straight for about 10 houses and then parts, creating two more streets, each going in opposite directions. The houses are made of wood and other natural materials, which make the place look a little old, as if they haven't renovated for a while.

As I look around, I see what looks to be regular people. The only thing that gives away the fact that they are not is what some of them are doing. There is a little crowd of people surrounding a man and woman, who are dancing while waving fire around in the air. Wait. They are not holding something that is on fire—their *hands* are *on* fire. They show no sign of pain; in fact they are laughing and having fun as the crowd claps and cheers them on.

I also notice the difference in clothing. I wear everyday clothes, which consist of blue jeans, a purple T-shirt and black boots. They are wearing very exotic and beautiful clothing that flows nicely around them, making them look elegant and magical. The women wear bright red, yellow or orange dresses, some with white tops and a corset to match the skirt, and others with a small top that covers their chests and a skirt. Some wear tops with tight black pants. None of them wear shoes. The men wear black pants and a red, yellow or orange vest or muscle top and black boots. None of the outfits have long sleeves, leaving their arms bare so I can see the tattoos of intricate yellow designs twisting up from their hands to their shoulders. The tattoos have an eerie glow to them.

My father clears his throat loudly, and everyone looks up at us and rushes forward to greet my parents.

Suddenly, the crowd separates, leaving room for a powerful-looking man to come through. I'm guessing by his posture and stance that he's the King. His clothes resemble the others'. The only difference is that he has tattoos over every visible part of his body; he even has them outlining his face. Some of his short brown hair covers a bit of them. He looks about my parents' age. He continues forward and starts circling me, looking me over as though I was something to be bought. I stiffen and start to take a step back, but looks from my parents hold me in place. During those long minutes, I feel intimidated and a bit violated. Finally he finishes his evaluation; the expression on his face doesn't give any clues to whether he is satisfied. He starts walking away and gestures for my parents to follow him. Before they follow him, they order me to stay behind, leaving me standing there awkwardly.

After they leave, the rest of the people take their turn to look me over. I avoid eye contact and do my best not to listen to their whispers.

Out of nowhere, a bell rings out. All the people around me run and form a single-file line. Unsure of what to do, I just stand there. I see my parents running towards me, and they grab and pull me behind the line of people.

From where I stand, the figure approaching us is unmistakable: it is the man from the locked room, the one I accidentally let out. The men and women in front of me move forward and start throwing fire at him. He fights back, but they easily capture him, considering he is alone against an army of . . . whatever they are. They roughly tie him up and lead him into a building I hadn't noticed before; it is small and off to the side. It blends in with the scenery, with plants and vines growing all around it. The doors have giant locks on them, and the windows are made of metal bars.

As he walks directly past me, I think I see a small, devious smile flit across his lips, but it might just be a twitch. I can't detect any fear in his expression. They shove him in the building and lock the door. Two men stay behind to act as guards.

My parents lead me to another building, equally camouflaged and not too far from what I assume is the village prison. Once we are inside what I assume is my bedroom for my stay, I turn to face them.

"What just happened?" I demand. "And please, I want the full explanation this time."

They sigh in unison. My father is the first one to speak. "We already told you. We are the Fire Populous, and he's a very powerful Fire Demon." I have a million questions by now, but I decide to start off with the most immediate one. "Are you going to lock him up forever?"

"Yes, we will be keeping him locked up here for the rest of his life."

"Why didn't you just lock him up here in the first place?" I ask.

"Because, your mother and I wanted to keep a close eye on him."

"What did he do, before, when you first locked him up?"

Father pauses. "He, um, killed a Fire Populous."

"Get some rest," my mother says. "You have a long day ahead of you tomorrow. Everyone around here has to pull her own weight."

"Just one more question," I say. "Can I do . . . that?"

"Do what?"

"The fire thing," I say.

"Yes, we already told you this," she replies. "But you can't use it yet—you need to be trained."

"So you'll train me?"

"Of course. Your training will start tomorrow."

I tell myself I'm not excited, but deep down I know I am. I don't want to admit that I'm not a human, that I'm some creature that can wield fire. Although it's really cool, I thought stuff like that only happens in movies or fairy tales. I look outside and realize it's already dark, so I decide it's time for bed. Tomorrow will be a big day.

CHAPTER 3

J awake the next day thinking, *What a weird dream I had!* I open my eyes to see I'm in a hut with yellow walls and light hardwood floor. The bed I'm lying in looks strangely like the one from my so-called dream. I get up and take a shower, and in that shower is when I make the mental click: last night's dream was *not* a dream.

I put on the clothes I find waiting for me on the bed, and I look into the bathroom mirror. With the tight black pants, white top and yellow vest I am wearing, I now look more like the other Fire Populous. The only thing missing is the tattoos.

I head downstairs and see my parents sitting at a table eating breakfast; they are wearing Fire Populous clothing now as well. We eat breakfast in silence. When we finish eating, they tell me they will start me off with a simple job: cut away the plants and vines around the prison. They don't want the Fire Demon using them for anything dangerous. They give me some gardening shears and send me out to work. I must admit, I am a little nervous to go to the prison. Those nerves subside a little as I see the two guards at the door. I decide to start at the side and work my way around.

I start cutting the plants, and then I hear a soft yet confident and slightly condescending voice say, "Sorry about yesterday. No hard feelings, right?" I look up to see the man who attacked me yesterday, looking at me through the bars on the window. I ignore him and do not reply as

I continue cutting the plants. He says, "Ah, the silent treatment. Two can play at this game." He is silent for approximately five seconds. Then, "What do they think I'll do with those vines? Sharpen them and use them for spears? I'm good, but I'm not that good."

I roll my eyes. "What happened to the silent treatment?" I ask.

"Ah! She speaks! And besides, I don't need vines to get out. I could easily get out any time I wanted."

"Then why are you still here?" I ask.

"Because I haven't felt like escaping yet," he says arrogantly.

"Whatever," I reply as I go back to my work.

"You know," he starts up again, "it would be a lot faster if you burnt them. Oh right, you can't."

"Careful—I have shears," I warn him.

"Feisty little one, aren't you? So when did they say your lessons start? Today, isn't it?"

"None of your business."

"I'm right, aren't I? They told you it would start today. But what's really starting is the brainwashing process."

"How would you know?"

"That's for me to know, and you not to."

I sigh and walk away. I'll finish cutting the weeds later. This guy is obviously untrustworthy. First he tries to kill me, and then he gets all buddy-buddy with me? I don't think so. He likely wants to trick me into helping him escape. How stupid does he think I am?

I leave to find my parents and ask them about the class. They direct me to the location, and I try to sneak in without being noticed. I've always hated being the new kid. Although it doesn't happen very often, it still scares me.

Even though I'm quiet, everyone stares at me as I sit down, and then I realize why. Not only am I the last to arrive and the new kid, but they also all have their intricate yellow tattoos spiraling up their arms, and I do not.

"Everybody, this is Rosalie," the teacher announces.

"Everyone calls me Rose," I say.

"All right then, Rose. Rule number one: Stay away from water. I'm not sure if you've already learnt this the hard way, but water for us is like fire for humans and other Populous: It stings us and hurts very badly. It leaves burns and scars. It can also kill you, if you are in it for too long. If you ever happen to touch water, we have a special healing salve that reverses its effects almost immediately. Rule number two: Always take your pills after class; they help you control your powers. Rule number three: All spell books are off limits to everyone but the King. If we catch you with one, the punishment will be severe."

"We have spell books?" I blurt out before I can stop myself. I cringe when all eyes turn back to me.

"Yes, we do. The spells and potions in there are very powerful and can do almost anything, but they are easily taken advantage of, and therefore no one may use them unless given permission from the King. Now, we'll start with a basic exercise. Everyone, gather in a circle and concentrate on making a flame in your hand. While keeping it under control, move it around in the palm of your hand. Rose, since you're new and have never used your powers before, you can start by igniting your finger."

By the end of the morning, I only manage to heat up the very tip of my index. Everyone else has nearly perfected making the flames in their hands.

The teacher lets everyone go home for a lunch break with instructions to come back for afternoon classes. I'm not hungry, and I figure it's a good idea to finish cutting the weeds. I hope he won't talk to me again, but soon enough I hear him.

"By the way, I'm Seth. And you are?"

I ignore him.

"So what's your favourite colour?"

I grit my teeth and continue to say nothing.

"Favourite food? Season? Sport?"

He goes on like this for about five minutes until my will breaks. "My name is Rose. Why do you care, anyway?"

"Rose. What a nice name. Like the flower, I presume?"

Knowing he won't give me a straight answer, I leave again.

I go back to afternoon classes, which are academic. Today it's math, followed by history and biology. Afterwards, the teacher passes out little pills to everyone and stands over us to make sure we swallow them.

I swallow my pill and feel it go down. Immediately I feel different. It feels harder to concentrate, as if the pill is doing something to my mind, not my powers.

I go back to the prison to finish my job.

"How was class?" Seth asks.

I don't answer. I really can't take much more of this.

"Did you take your pills like a good little girl?"

"Actually, yeah. How do you know about that?"

"You don't answer any of my questions, so why should I answer yours?"

"Fine. It's not like I care, anyways."

I storm away, putting off my job once again.

The next morning, I confront my parents about when we're leaving. They glance at each other nervously.

"Actually, Sweetie," Mom begins. "We can't go back now that you know everything. We can't risk anyone finding out about this."

SHAYLYNN WILBON

I am speechless. Not that I hate it here, but I don't like the idea of being trapped. My parents exit the room, leaving me alone with my thoughts. *What about Macy and Adam? Will I ever see them again? What will they think has happened to me?*

I decide that I will quickly finish cutting those stupid plants before class starts. I start cutting them, and of course Seth shows up at the window.

"I see you're almost done with the weeds."

I ignore him and continue cutting. The sooner I finish, the better.

"Have you been to the beach yet? It's quite nice. Just don't go in the water!" he goads.

I refuse to take the bait and continue cutting. *Almost done. I can get through this. I will get through this.* I cut the last weed and with a sigh of relief go to my morning classes.

The morning passes pretty much the same as last time, but my finger gets a little bit hotter. I think. The rest of the students have already formed fireballs in their hands.

After morning class, I eat lunch by myself, go to afternoon classes and take my pill. Again, after I swallow the pill, my mind feels hazy, and I can't seem to concentrate so well. It's almost as if my mind is not completely my own. I decide to try to sleep it off. It's probably happening because I'm not used to it yet.

The rest of the week passes in pretty much the same way. Now that I'm not going near the prison for weeding, I must admit, I kind of miss Seth's incessant chatting. He's the only person, other than my parents with whom I've had a real conversation. That thought scares me. I can't like him. He's a prisoner. Not only that, he's a demon, a murderer. Regrettably, I feel a pang of sadness. I will myself to stop it. He's the enemy; he's obviously done some pretty bad stuff. I don't care if they lock him up for the rest of his life. I don't. Really.

That day after class, I find myself with a lot of free time. I decide to go check out the beach Seth was talking about. Although, not because he suggested it, of course.

I'm walking down the beach when I see a figure in the distance. Curious, I walk towards it. It's the unmistakeable tall, lean, imposing figure of Seth. Seeing him again like this brings back fear from the first encounter. Something tells me to run, but I can't give him that satisfaction.

I bravely look up at him. "How did you get out?"

He laughs. "I told you I could do it anytime I wanted."

"I'm going to tell the Fire Populous," I announce as I turn away.

He grabs my arm to stop me, saying, "Wait!"

Feeling his touch on my arm, a jolt of fear goes through me, and I turn around. I know it is showing in my eyes, because when I meet his gaze, I see regret in his eyes, and he lets go of my arm. Regret for scaring me? No, that can't be it.

"Let me explain." He pauses. "Please." He is gazing at me in a way that makes me unable to say no.

"Fine, make it quick."

"One day my parents and I were sailing home after doing some research on the Fire Demons, trying to see how bad they really are."

"Wait, aren't you a Fire Demon?"

"Just let me finish," he says. "Out of nowhere, a bunch of fireballs started flying towards our boat. Our ship set on fire and started sinking. We had to jump ship. I'm not sure how I made it back to the island, but I did. My parents weren't so lucky. I confronted the Fire Populous, and they locked me up. I was only 15 at the time. I had no idea what was going on, but being in that prison all day, I found that my mind was becoming clearer than before. I was able to concentrate better. I realized the only thing that was really different was that I wasn't taking those pills anymore. I figured out that the little pills they gave us after school were actually to brainwash us. I'm not sure why, but I know they've been doing it for some time now, because the process is slow—or at least it *was* slow, they may have found a way to speed it up over the years. Anyways, because my parents were researchers, there was a small possibility they could have found out about this. The chance was small, but still a big enough threat to have to kill them." He looks away angrily, and I feel a small stab of pity before I stop myself. He's just a talented smooth talker trying to get out of a really big mess.

"You don't believe me, do you?" he asks.

"Well, no," I confirm.

He continues anyway. "Then when they found out what I knew, they locked me up in that room."

"Wait, the room in my house?" I ask incredulously.

"Yes. They only slipped food and water through the door. So when the door opened all the way, I didn't know what was happening, and I freaked out. I thought someone might be coming to kill me."

"Okay . . . Then why did you come after us?"

"Because I didn't want you to tell the rest of the Fire Populous that I had escaped."

"Okay . . ." I repeat. "Then why did you continue to follow us when we got to the island?"

"Because I felt like it. Enough with the questions!"

"I still don't believe you. My parents would never do anything like that!"

"Are you sure about that?"

That strikes a nerve. He can't just go around accusing my parents like this! "You could never be a Fire Populous! You're nothing but a stupid, evil, little Fire Demon!"

By the look in his eyes, I figure I too have struck a nerve. He angrily holds his arm out and yanks his red shirt sleeve back to reveal a tattoo. I peer closer and recognize it to be the same tattoo I have seen on the other Fire Populous. It takes a moment for me to process this. All I can do is stare for a few seconds.

"You could have gotten that anywhere," I say unconvincingly.

"No, I couldn't have. If I had gotten it anywhere else other than here, it wouldn't glow the way it does. The only way for it to glow like this is by having it done with a special kind of ink enchanted with magic, from the spell books of the king himself," Seth replies. "Now do you believe me?"

I'm speechless for a moment. Then I whisper, "Yes."

"Finally. Now, I've got to go before the guards come check on me again, but remember—don't take your pill!"

He turns and walks away. I watch him leave and then collapse in the sand. I can't take all this in. My parents would never do something like this . . . but he had a lot of proof, and the tattoo. I've lived with my parents all my life—how could I not know anything about this? But I suppose that would show how good they are at keeping secrets. I guess there's only one thing to do. I won't take the pill, and I'll see what happens.

Chapter 4

The next morning I wake up and prepare myself for my morning classes. I'm nervous for what will happen today, and I barely slept all night. I was too busy thinking about what happened and what Seth told me. I try to stop thinking about it and go to my class. Once again, I make next to no progress. After class, I eat lunch and return for my academic classes. At the end of the class, the teacher comes around with the pills. As he gets closer, I start to get nervous. What if he can tell I didn't swallow it? What if I spit it out? What if I actually swallow it? The teacher walks over to my desk, hands me my pill and a glass of juice, and stands over me, waiting for me to swallow it. I take the pill, put it in my mouth, take the juice and put some in my mouth and swallow the liquid, making sure the pill doesn't go down with it. When he's gone, I hide the pill in my pocket and get up and leave. After supper I go to the beach, but I'm not hoping Seth's going to be there or anything—at least that's what I keep telling myself.

I get to the beach just as the sun is setting. I don't see him, but I'm not disappointed. I sit down in the sand by the water, making sure not to touch it. I sit here for a few minutes and then hear a rustling in the trees. I look to the right, and there's nothing beside me. I look to the left, and Seth's sitting right beside me.

"I didn't take the pill," I say.

"Good," he says.

"So, what now?" I ask.

"Well," he says, looking uncharacteristically shy. "I could, um, show you how to use your powers, I guess."

"Okay," I say, feeling equally shy.

"Think of something that makes you really mad. Sadly, that's where our power comes from—anger."

I focus on everything I feel towards my parents, the betrayal and confusion, and the feeling that I don't know them anymore.

"So what are you thinking of?" he asks.

"You," I retort.

He is quiet and then says, "Focus on your anger to set your hand on fire."

"I can't believe I'm actually trying to set my hand on fire," I say.

He lets out a little laugh. "Just do it."

I close my eyes, focusing on my anger and concentrate on setting my hand on fire. Suddenly my hand feels warm. I open my eyes. It's on fire! A huge smile spreads across my face, and without thinking, I jump into Seth's arms and hug him. I close my eyes, thinking, *This feels kind of nice.* Then I realize who it is, and my eyes pop open immediately. I pull back quickly and can feel my cheeks burning. I wouldn't be surprised if they were on fire, too. We both start getting up, and I babble something about being sorry. Then he starts taking off his shirt, and I wonder, *What is he doing?*

He must have seen the confused look on my face because he explains, "You set it on fire."

"Oh," I say. Then I realize my hand is still on fire. I concentrate on putting it out, and it works. As he puts out the fire on his shirt, I apologize again, this time about his shirt. I notice there's not much damage to it. I decide it would be best if I left now.

I say one last "sorry" and then say good-bye. I get out of there before I embarrass myself even further.

"Good-bye," he calls after me. "Oh, and I like your necklace by the way!"

I clutch my necklace in my hand. He must know what it does and I'm not sure if that's a good thing or a bad thing.

I get back to my room and start thinking about what just happened. I still can't believe I did that! As I'm pondering it, I realize that he didn't even hug me back! Either he didn't like it, or he was too shocked to return it. But it doesn't matter, because I tell myself I didn't like it, either.

To get my mind off things, I take a burning hot shower and then go to bed.

The next morning, I wake up and go to my classes, and then the dreaded lunch time arrives. Everybody else has already gone with their friends, and here I am, alone. Without even thinking, I start walking towards the prison. I arrive there and walk towards the window where Seth usually is. I walk up to the window and look in. I see Seth sitting by himself, all alone in one of the corners of the cell. He has his shirt back on, and I notice with relief it only looks a little bit charred.

Why did I come here? I think to myself. *This is so stupid. I'd rather eat by myself.* I start walking away, but I hear his voice calling my name.

"Rose! Couldn't stay away, could you?"

I cringe and slowly turn around. I sigh and mumble quietly, "Is it okay if I eat here?"

"What was that?" I repeat it, but still quietly. "What?"

"Is it okay if I eat here?" I yell.

"Sure," he says, and he grabs the bars. Before I can realize what's happening, they're bent and he's climbing out.

"What if someone sees you?" I ask.

"I think you should be more worried about whether or not someone sees *you*," he says with a smirk.

We walk over more into the trees and sit down. Suddenly I feel really shy. I lay out my lunch bag and take out an apple. I bring it towards my mouth, getting ready to bite it, and then he grabs it out of my hand and takes a bite. I glare at him.

"What?" he says. "It's the first decent food I've had all week!"

I roll my eyes, take out a sandwich and unwrap it. Before I can bite it, he takes that, too.

"Got anything else in there?" he asks.

"Actually, I do," I reply. "And it's for *me*."

I pull out the granola bar, and before I can even unwrap it, he grabs it from my hand.

"Hey!" I yell.

"What are you going to do about it?" he asks as he starts to unwrap it.

"This!" I yell, and I pounce on him, trying to grab it back. He's holding it out of my reach and trying to push me off him, but I can tell that he's trying to make sure he doesn't hurt me. Can't say I'm doing the same. As we are laughing and wrestling for the food, I hear footsteps in the bush.

Somebody appears through the trees and sees me lying on top of the prisoner on the island. I realize how bad that looks. Before I can say anything, he turns and runs, probably for backup.

"Oh shit!" Seth swears.

I quickly get off of him. Before we can think of a plan, there's a bunch of Fire Populous surrounding us.

"Oh shit indeed," I mutter.

The guards grab us, but before they can grab Seth, he whispers in my ear.

"Don't worry; I'll get us out of this."

Then he fights off some guards and disappears into the woods. Most of the guards run after him, and some start bringing me back, probably to my parents.

I can see my parents standing by the house that we're staying at. They have extremely angry looks on their faces. They say nothing and start leading me towards the prison. I follow in confusion. Once we get to the door, the guards open it and shove me in.

"What is going on?" I yell. "Why are you locking me in here?"

My parents don't reply and walk away, leaving me alone in the prison. I walk to the corner that I saw Seth sitting in earlier today. I sit down, bring my knees up to my chest and rest my head on my knees.

They leave me there for hours. Outside, it's getting dark. Then I hear the guards opening the door. They walk in, pull me up off the floor—not very gently—and drag me outside. They are joined by more guards and continue to drag me now through the trees to the beach, where my parents are waiting.

"What's going on?" I ask them.

They don't reply. After about 10 minutes of walking, we suddenly stop at a dock. It is now dark out. The other people with us form a circle around us and look our way. My father starts speaking to the people around us.

"It is a sad day when we find our own daughter with the prisoner, and sadly for that she must be punished. And so, in the presence of you all, we will do exactly that. Since consorting with the enemy is one of the worst crimes, she must be punished with the most severe method."

My parents unlatch the clasp of my necklace and take it off, then the guards who were walking with us grab me by the wrists. Then they lift me and dunk me into the water, with only my wrists and hands sticking out. At first I don't understand what is happening. It doesn't hurt. Then suddenly I feel this wave of pain. I let out a cry, and with it the air in my lungs.

The pain I feel is so fierce that it feels as if I am burning to death. *How could my parents do this to me? I'm their daughter!* I think to myself.

Suddenly the hands let go, and I start sinking to the bottom. I try to propel myself up. I kick and I push with my hands, trying to reach the top, but it hurts so much, and I'm getting nowhere. Just as I think I'm gone for sure, I feel a pair of hands grabbing me again.

They pull me up out of the water, and the next thing I know, I'm being cradled in someone's arms. Whoever's holding me starts running. As I'm being carried, I'm coughing and trying to catch my breath. I look up and see Seth's face.

"I thought I told you not to go swimming," he says with that unforgettable smirk on his face.

I roll my eyes, but I can't help smiling a little. Then I cringe because of the pain that little movement causes.

"It's okay," he says. "I have some of that healing salve with me. Just hold on."

After another little while, I ask, "How long have we been running?"

"You mean how long have *I* been running."

"Yeah, whatever. How long have *you* been running?"

"About a half hour," he says. "We're almost at the boats they have on the other side of the island."

Half an hour? I think. He's been carrying me and running through the trees for half an hour? And it doesn't even feel like he's been slowing down.

He runs for a little while longer, and we reach the boats. He puts me in one, gets in and unties the boat from the dock. Then he starts the motor and drives us away.

As he's driving, I see my parents, followed by a bunch of guards, racing out from the forest.

"Is there anything I can do?" I ask Seth.

"No," he says.

"Are you sure?" I ask.

"You'll only slow us down," he says rudely.

Then they start throwing fireballs at us.

"On second thought," he says. "I need you to start throwing fireballs at *them*."

"I thought you didn't need my help," I shoot back.

"Just hurry up and do it!"

"But I'll only slow you down, remember?"

"Just do it!"

"What's the magic word?"

"Please," he snaps.

"Say it like you mean it."

Seth looks from the people following us (who are now getting into their own boats) to my eyes, and he says very softly, "Please, Rose."

I feel a shiver go through me. I hope he didn't see it. "Sure, I'll do it," I say. "Just one thing—I don't know how."

"Just think of all the betrayal you must be feeling right now, and put your arm out. Then try to feel the anger surge through your arm and out your fingertips."

It sounds kind of doubtful to me, but I do as he says, because it's a matter of life and death. I sit up, close my eyes and focus on the betrayal that I feel. The burning pain I feel all over my body helps me with that. All of a sudden I feel heat surge down my arm into my hand, and then it's gone. I open my eyes, and I see a fireball hit something!

Out of excitement, I yell, "Oh my God, I did it!"

"Yeah you did," he says. "Now *keep* doing it!"

I'm still not sure how, but I do. Seth keeps driving. Before I know it, we've struck land. Seth pulls the boat into some bushes and reaches out to carry me again.

"No, it's okay," I say.

"Trust me, it's not. It may not feel like it yet, but your body is still in shock." And with that, he scoops me up and runs into the trees, leaving our followers behind. He runs for about five minutes and then sits me down at a fallen tree trunk.

"We'll set up camp here for the night," he says.

"But won't they find us?" I ask.

"This is Water Populous territory. They won't dare come here," he answers.

"Can I have that healing salve now?" I ask, still feeling the burning all over my body.

"Here." Seth hands it to me. "Put it on all over."

I stand up to go into the forest and put on the healing salve, but my legs go numb. I fall, and Seth catches me before I can hit the ground.

"Careful," he says as he sets me back down on the log. "I'll go collect wood in the forest for a while. Call when you're done."

"Okay," I say, and I wait until he is out of sight. When he is, I take off my clothes and apply the salve. When I see myself, I pray that this salve will quickly heal these ugly burns. Once I'm done applying the salve, I put on my clothes, relieved that the pain is gone. When my clothes are on, I call for Seth to come back.

He returns and drops a pile of wood on the ground. I hand Seth the rest of the healing salve, and he rubs it on his hands and forearms, which must have gotten wet when he pulled me out.

"So where do we go from here?" I ask.

"*I* am going to find an Air Populous and ask her for help. I don't know where *you're* going."

I decide to ignore that last bit for now and ask him, "Why do you need help?"

"Do you seriously know nothing about the four elements? The Air Populous can speak to the spirits in the wind. I'm going to get one to help me talk to my parents." There's an uncharacteristic sadness in his eyes, but he hides it right away and starts stacking the wood for the fire.

He finishes gathering and starts the fire. It is now dark out, and I'm really tired.

I ask, "So what am I supposed to sleep on?"

He laughs. "Sorry, Princess, but we don't have anything to sleep on. This isn't exactly a five-star hotel."

"Well, it should be!" I finish lamely.

Seth rolls his eyes and lies down by the fire. I get up off the log and lie down on the other side of the fire. I fall asleep as soon as I close my eyes.

CHAPTER 5

The next day I wake up wondering where I am. Then I remember the events of yesterday. Tears come to my eyes, and I wonder, *What am I supposed to do now?* I look down at my hands and arms: all of my burns and scars from being in the water yesterday are gone. I look around some more to see that the fire is out and that Seth is still asleep on the other side of it.

In sleep, Seth looks peaceful and doesn't have that arrogant look on his face. I actually kind of like him—when he's asleep. Something about the innocence of his features draws me in, so I move closer to get a better look. As I'm crouching down beside him, I can't help but reach out one hand. Just as I'm lightly running my fingers over his cheek, his eyes snap open.

I jump back, feeling my cheeks burning red. "I, um, I was just—sorry. That was weird. I don't even know what I was doing . . . Bug! There was a bug!"

"You just couldn't resist, could you?" he says, stifling a laugh.

I'm too embarrassed to say anything. Seth then gets up and starts walking into the forest.

"Where are you going?" I yell after him.

"I already told you where I'm going yesterday," he tosses back.

"To find the Air Populous?" I ask.

"No, to find Santa Claus."

"Why can't I come?"

"Because I'm too old for babysitting."

"I'm the same age as you!"

"Really?" he asks. "I'd never have guessed it."

"Why are you so mean?"

"Why are *you* still here?"

"You can't just leave me here!"

"I can, and I will."

I reach out and grab his arm to stop him. He turns around and gives me this annoyed, tired look. I almost let go, but I don't.

"Please," I beg. "I need you and you need me."

"Um, no," he answers. "I don't really need you, actually."

"Please, I'll keep quiet." *Most of the time*, I think to myself. "And I won't bug you!" *A lot.*

"Fine." He sighs, shakes my arm off of him and continues on.

After a few minutes of walking in silence, I hear rustling in the bushes. Seth must hear it too, because he immediately faces the bushes, grabs my arm and pulls me behind him protectively. With one hand still around my arm, he listens.

We hear the rustling in the bushes again. There's shaking, and out pop three people. I'm guessing they're Water Populous, considering we're on their island. Plus, they have intricate tattoos spiraling up from their hands to their shoulders, just like the Fire Populous but blue. They also wear the same type of clothing as the Fire Populous, but instead of red, yellow or orange, they wear various shades of blue.

Then the big bulky one with short dark brown hair, tan skin and brown eyes—and did I mention he was really tall?—starts flinging balls of water at us.

Seth moves us both out of the way before they hit us, and he throws a fireball at him. The fireball hits him and sends him flying. He hits his head on a tree and falls to the ground. He doesn't get up and his head rests at an odd angle. His eyes are closed. Then the tall and scrawny one with blonde hair and green eyes steps in, and Seth does the same with him. The third guy, short but muscular, runs away. Seth lets out a low laugh.

"Come on! Let's go!" Seth says, grabbing my arm and pulling me deeper into the forest.

"Did you . . . ?" I can't finish the sentence.

"Kill them? Yes," he answers with no emotion.

"How did you kill them so easily? It was three against two!" I say.

"You mean one?"

"Whatever. How did you do it?"

"I was able to do it because I'm awesome."

I roll my eyes but say nothing. We walk in silence for a few minutes. I decide to break it. "How did you get your tattoo? Is it a permanent tattoo? Did they brand you? Is it washable?"

He laughs at me and rolls his eyes. "It's a permanent tattoo that you get when you turn 13. If you prove you're worthy of one, that is."

Chapter 6

"Where are we going?" I ask.

"The Fire Populous will be circling the island for a while. We are waiting until they give up or assume we were killed by the Water Populous and go back to the Fire Populous island. Then we can get back on the boat and go to the Air Populous' island without being attacked when we get off of the island," Seth answers.

We continue to walk until we are back at the beach from where we came. The Fire Populous' boats are gone. Seth pulls our boat out of the bushes and puts it back in the water, and then we get in. He starts the motor and drives us away from the island.

After only a few minutes, the motor stops working. "We're out of gas," Seth says. He takes the oars that are on the floor of the boat and starts rowing. "So," Seth begins, and then he snickers. "So," he tries again. "What was it like, growing up as a . . ." He struggles to get it out. "Human!" He bursts out laughing like it's the funniest thing he's ever heard.

I couldn't tell Seth how I only had two friends back home, so I say, "It was great! I was so popular and had so many friends at school. I had trouble leaving them all. Then I met you, and everything went downhill from there."

"Ha ha," he replies. "You can leave at anytime, you know. And by the way, I believe it was you who practically begged to come along with me."

"Doesn't mean I enjoy it," I mutter.

He continues rowing in silence after that, and my mind starts to wander. Seth is so arrogant and cocky! All he talks about is how he's so amazing and how everybody else sucks! Like it's such an honour to be in his presence! He's one of those types: he's hot and he knows it! Maybe he's used to girls falling all over him, but no self-respecting person would ever go for a guy like that.

"I'm sorry you had to leave all your friends," he says suddenly. I look up in surprise and search his face, but I don't see any arrogance in his features. "I know I miss all of my friends. I obviously haven't seen them in a long time."

"Um, thanks," I reply hesitantly, waiting for the punch line. None comes. Instantly, it's awkward again. I almost wish he hadn't shown that little bit of emotion.

Breaking the silence, he asks, "What is it exactly that humans do?"

"Well," I begin. "We eat grass, drink water from the lake, and walk around naked in public. Oh, and we dance around the fire at night. Sometimes we even sacrifice animals!"

"Really?" he leans forward, fascinated.

"No! We aren't crazy people! We're just like you, except we don't throw fire all over the place."

"Funny how you say 'you.' So, do you consider yourself a Fire Populous or a human? Do you *miss* the human world? Do you wish you could go back?" All the excitement drains from his face, replaced with that arrogant look that I've come to know so well.

"In some ways I'm human, and in some ways I'm a Fire Populous! Sometimes I want to go back, and sometimes I don't!"

"Why do you want to go back?"

"You!"

He smirks. "And why do you want to stay?"

You. I think, but don't answer. I push the thought away, horrified. The stress must be getting to me. He gives a cocky little smile as if he knows exactly what I'm thinking. I look away and ask, "Are we there yet?"

"Do you see an island?" he demands.

"No."

"Then we're not there yet."

I give him a dirty look, and we continue in silence.

Soon I see an island in the distance. "We're almost there!" I say.

"I've been rowing this whole time, so you can row the rest of the way." He throws the oars to me. To my intense embarrassment, I drop them.

"Look what you did!" he exclaims angrily. "Well, I guess you're pulling the boat to shore. I knew I shouldn't have brought you!"

"I'm so sorry! But what do we do now?"

"Like I said, you're gonna have to pull the boat back, 'cause I'm not going in."

"Seth, I can't go back in there!"

I see his hard eyes soften briefly. He takes off his shirt and starts rowing with it. We barely move, so he tries to reach for the oar with his shirt. He manages to finally get it back to us.

"Now don't drop it!" he scolds.

I take the oar without saying anything, thankful that I don't have to go in the water.

He reaches out for the other oar with his shirt and retrieves it. Then he throws his shirt into the water. "What?" He asks, seeing the questioning expression on my face. "It's full of water. I'm not putting it back on!"

Seth takes the oars and finishes rowing us to the island.

We get off the boat and onto the island.

"So this is the Air Populous' island?" I ask.

"Yeah," Seth replies as he pulls the boat further onto the shore. Once he's finished, he starts walking through the forest, towards the Air Populous.

"Um, we aren't enemies with the Air Populous, are we?" I ask.

"No," he replies, "We are allied with the Air Populous."

"Oh. So who are we going to ask for help? Are you friends with an Air Populous?"

"I thought you said you weren't going to bother me, if I let you come with me," he retorts.

"Fine, don't answer me," I mumble. I cross my arms and continue to follow him, already frustrated with him after only two seconds of talking to him.

We walk in silence, passing nothing but trees for what seems like forever. When we finally arrive at what I hope is our final destination, a beautiful, tall, thin girl who looks to be about my age comes running out of a house to greet us. She has hair so fair and blonde that it almost looks white. The way she wears her long hair down makes it almost look like its floating around her, caressing her face and softening her beautiful facial features. Her pale skin and stunning blue eyes make her look both innocent and wise, as though she's seen all there is to see and knows all there is to know. Her blue flowing dress hugs her body and shows how tiny and fragile she is. The colour of her dress only intensifies her pale skin and blue eyes. Her white tattoos make her skin look even more fair and translucent.

Once she arrives, she immediately takes Seth into a huge embrace. In return Seth lifts her up off the ground and spins her around. I feel a pang of jealousy that I try to shake off but can't. *Why am I feeling this way about her? I don't like him! Why do I care if they hug?*

"I've missed you so much," he tells her. Again I feel another pang of jealousy towards this girl. I'm not sure what has come over me.

"I can't believe you're finally free," she says, practically sobbing.

"How did you know I was locked up?" Seth asks.

"Your parents told me," Maria says.

Seth puts her down and motions towards me. "This is Rose; she's the one who freed me."

"I can't possibly thank you enough," she says to me, giving me such a beautiful, genuine, kind smile that I can't help but feel guilty for the jealousy I'm feeling.

Seth introduces us. "Rose, this is Maria. We were very close friends before . . . well, you know."

"Nice to meet you," I say. I try to give her a smile as beautiful and genuine as hers, but I probably failed miserably.

"Please come in, have something to eat and drink and get cleaned up and out of those filthy clothes," Maria says, leading us into her small, magical-looking home. "You can hide here."

"Hide here?" I repeat.

"Rose, the Fire Populous will no doubt be after us," Seth says.

"Oh, right," I say.

Once inside, Maria tells Seth to go get cleaned up and ready for dinner, while she helps me do the same. She leads me up a winding staircase to what I assume is her room. It is a very sophisticated and grownup-looking room. Its pale blue walls and bedspread make the room very cozy, and her boudoir has all sorts of makeup and jewelry on it. Her brown shelves are full of books and little trinkets, like snow globes and music boxes, and her closet is full of long and flowing gowns, most of them blue. She leads me through a door and into the bathroom.

"You can take a shower and get ready in here. Feel free to use whatever you want, including makeup and jewelry. I'll leave some clothes on the bed for you, and when you're done getting cleaned up, just come downstairs. Then I'll take you to the dining room. All right?" she asks with that beautiful smile plastered on her face.

"Um, yeah, thanks," I mumble, feeling suddenly very self-conscious in her presence.

I skip the shower because it's a water shower and I no longer have my necklace to protect me from the pain of water, and then I do my hair. After that I head into Maria's room and put on the clothes she left out for me. When I'm done getting ready, I look at myself in the mirror. What I see isn't as bad as I was expecting, however it does not even compare to the innocent beauty that is Maria. I see an okay-looking girl with brown, wavy hair and dark brown eyes, wearing a beautiful blue strapless dress. I'm guessing Maria doesn't own any red, yellow or orange.

Thinking this'll have to do, I walk downstairs. Maria is there to lead me to the dining room like she promised.

Once at the door, Maria motions me in. "I'm sorry, but you and Seth will be dining alone tonight. I have some things to sort out." She winks at me and gives me a knowing look.

I blink in confusion and enter the dining room, where Seth is waiting. As soon as I walk in, he looks at me with a surprised look on his face. He slowly looks me over, and his surprised look turns into an impressed look, but just as quickly as the look appears, it's gone, replaced by his usual, arrogant expression. "Wow, you look almost as good as I do," he says with a smirk.

I roll my eyes and sit down in the seat beside him; unfortunately, it's the only other seat in the room. I must admit he does look good in black pants, white T-shirt and blue vest. I think to myself and blush, even though I didn't say it out loud.

I look at the food placed out in front of me and start eating, savouring every bite of the potatoes, vegetables and lasagna. I hadn't even realized how hungry I was until now. Seth is digging into his food, which tells me he is feeling the same way.

After we finish eating and drinking literally everything that was laid out before us, we sit there in awkward silence, neither of us sure what to say or do.

"So, did you ask Maria about talking to your parents yet?" I ask, breaking the silence.

"No, I haven't had the chance to yet," Seth replies.

"You and Maria were friends growing up?" I ask, trying to get a real conversation going.

"Yeah, she was and still is one of my best friends. But don't worry." He smirks at me in the way he always does when he's about to say something he thinks is clever. "We're just friends, so there's no need to be jealous."

I glare at him and say nothing, because even though I know he's not serious about knowing I was jealous, I do feel reassured—which sucks.

"What was it like being stuck in that room for so long?" I blurt out before I can stop myself.

Seth looks at me, as surprised by the sudden serious question as I am. Then his expression quickly turns to one of true sadness, making me regret ever asking it. "It was horrible. I couldn't see, I could barley move, and I had nothing to do but think. And for me, having all of that time to think was even more horrible. I'm surprised I didn't go crazy."

"How did you stay in such great shape?" I blurt out, and then I roll my eyes at myself. As if I need to build up his self-confidence and give him more reasons to be arrogant.

Seth smiles in satisfaction. "Well, I ran in place and did sit-ups and push-ups for hours at a time," he says.

"What did you think about?" I ask, again without really thinking.

Seth hesitates and then says, "Mostly about my parents and what happened to them. I spent most of my days trying to figure out how to escape, why I was in there and what was going on. I also wondered why they were still keeping me alive. Sometimes I wished they would just kill me already. Rose, you don't know what it was like, knowing they could kill you at any moment and hating yourself when you wanted them to do it."

I feel so sorry for what he has gone through, and I start to understand why he acts so arrogant and tough all the time. I wish I could ease his pain.

I grab his hand in mine and say, "I'm so sorry for what my parents put you through. I swear I didn't know about any of this."

All of a sudden I feel my body leaning in against my will. Unable to stop myself, I continue to lean closer and closer, my eyes slowly closing and my lips slowly parting. I see Seth doing the same. Our lips slowly get closer and closer, and my heart races faster and faster—until Maria comes in. We both jump apart, embarrassed and confused about what was just about to happen. The moment is now over, a thing of the past.

"I'm sorry to interrupt, but I just finished what I had to do, and I swear I had no idea that you two were about to . . ." Maria trails off.

"That's all right," Seth says. "I need to speak to you, anyways."

"What do you need?" Maria asks.

Seth clears his throat, "I was wondering if you could help me speak to my parents. There are some things I need to know."

"Of course. I'll try to contact them right now, if you'd like."

"I would, if you don't mind."

CHAPTER 7

*M*aria leads us into her living room and motions for us to sit on a beige leather sofa. While Maria takes a seat on a chair, moving in front of us, I take a quick look around. The walls of the living room are a burgundy red colour, and most of the furniture is beige like the sofa we are sitting on. The frames of her tables are brown and the surfaces are glass. She has a few potted plants here and there, and behind Maria is a big, flat-screen TV, which is surprising because she doesn't seem like the kind of person who would watch TV.

"Just give me a minute while I try to find their voices. It shouldn't be too hard—truthfully, they've been hanging around here ever since you guys arrived. I'm pretty sure your parents spirits have been following you this whole time, Seth," Maria says with a smile.

As Maria closes her eyes and tilts her head to the side, listening for the voices of Seth's parents, I lean towards Seth and whisper in his ear, "Can Maria only hear them? She can't see them?"

"Yeah, the Air Populous can only hear the spirits in the wind; they can't see them. Some Air Populous go crazy because of all of the voices they hear. They have methods to block them out, but it doesn't always work," he replies. "But there are legends about the—"

"I found them!" Maria exclaims, cutting off Seth.

"So do I just talk to them, or do you have to relay the message, or what?" Seth asks.

"All you have to do is talk and they'll hear. I'll have to tell you their response," Maria replies.

"All right. Well, I'm not quite sure where to start," Seth says, "There's so much I want to know."

"They said to take your time; they have all of eternity, after all," Maria says.

Seth lets out a little laugh. "I guess I'll start with: what did you find out that was so bad, they had to kill you to make sure no one else found out?"

"We found out that there really isn't such a thing as Fire Demons—it's just something the King came up with to keep the Fire Populous under control, to keep them from leaving or disobeying. The easiest way to control someone is to make them think you are protecting them from certain death," Maria says, now looking as if in a trance. It's as though Seth's parents are now controlling her words and her mind is elsewhere. "But that was just the beginning. After we found out about the Fire Demons not actually existing, we looked into it more. As it turned out, most of their so-called Fire Demons were former Fire Populous from the kingdom; they even had tattoos to prove it. They were said to have died or gotten lost or taken by the Fire Demons, but they had really been sent away into the jungle to fend for themselves and were never to return, or they would face the consequences, which was death."

"Why were they sent away?" Seth asks.

"Because they had begun to question whether there really was any danger. They had never seen any before, after all. Unfortunately for them, as soon as they started to question, they became a threat that needed to be gotten rid of."

"But why wouldn't they just kill them, make sure they would never be able to tell anyone?" Seth asks.

Seth's parents continue to talk through Maria. "It was your parents, Rose, who refused to kill them. At that point they were not yet completely brainwashed."

"Wait, what?" I ask, secretly proud that my parents did something right by not killing those Fire Populous, but also confused about the brainwashed part.

"We will get to that. You must be patient, Rose," they say. Both of Seth's parent's voices are now mixed together as they continue to speak to us through Maria, no longer using her voice. "We spoke to the 'Fire Demons,' and they all told us the same thing: there was some creature trying to control the King, and slowly but steadily it was succeeding. None of them knew how this was being done. They said the creature looks human like us and can wield fire like us, however when the Fire Demons spoke to the so-called Air Demons, they said they saw the same creature that could wield air. The Air Demons spoke to both the Earth Demons and the Water Demons who all reported seeing the same man wielding their element. What this means is that this man, this creature, can wield all four of the elements, which allows him to pretend to be a part of each kingdom."

"But how is that even possible?" Seth asks.

"Unfortunately, we do not know. They killed us before we could find out more," they say, their voices sounding regretful and sad.

Seth looks down at his hands, which he has balled into fists in his lap. He's clearly in pain and upset about the fact that his parents are dead, and he's trying to hide his pain by being strong, as usual.

"We know it is a lot to ask—and we know it will be very dangerous because we ended up dead trying to figure out what was going on—but we were wondering if you could continue our research and try to figure out what is going on. Please know that we would not ask this of you, if we did not think it is necessary. We believe that this man is after something, and we believe that he will stop at nothing to get it."

"All right, I'll do it," Seth says. "I just have one more question. Why didn't I die that night, when they sunk our ship?"

"We cast a spell, using spell books we found during one of our research trips," they say.

Seth waits for them to continue, and when they don't, he asks, "What kind of spell?"

Maria's body sighs. "We are very sorry for what we did, but we knew Rose's parents were going to come after us sooner or later, and we accepted it. But we couldn't let them get you, so we cast a spell that connected you to Rose. It made it so that if they killed you, she would die, too. We knew they wouldn't do that to their own daughter, so we cast the spell and left a note telling them what we had done, and then we left. Little did we know, they had a spell book as well. In that book was a spell that would erase one's memory. After they sunk our ship, when we were coming back to try to talk some sense into the rest of the Fire Populous, they used that spell on you, Rose, and took you and Seth to the house you were living in before you came here. You know the rest."

"Why would you do that?" I ask, "Now if they kill him, they kill me, too!"

"We are very sorry, but we didn't know what else to do."

"Rose, they were only trying to protect me," Seth says.

"Oh, we almost forgot: the only way to kill one of you without killing the other is if one of *you* kills the other." They pause and then say, "We must go now, but Seth, you must know that we love you, and we believe that you can do this."

"I love you, too, and I miss you. I'll try my best not to let you down."

Through Maria, Seth's parents stroke his cheek gently. Suddenly Maria stands up. She looks at us, her eyes no longer blank; Seth's parents are gone. "That was odd, that's never happened before, where the spirit takes over like that," she says.

"I'm going to go to bed now," Seth says, getting up and leaving abruptly.

"I think I will, too," I say as I stand up. "Where am I staying?"

"Follow me," Maria says. I'm lost in thought as Maria leads me to another room and then leaves.

I walk in and look around. This room has yellow walls, except the wall that the bed's headboard is against is purple. The bedspread is purple and yellow striped, and there is a pair of pajamas waiting for me. There is a light brown dresser and an empty closet on one wall and a light brown nightstand with a simple lamp and clock on it. The floor is covered in a white, shaggy carpet. After a long and hard day, I change into the pair of polka dot pajamas Maria left on the bed, get into the bed and fall asleep quickly.

The next day, I wake up and head to Maria's room. Before I can knock, she opens the door and gives me one of her smiles. "You can shower and change in here, and then meet Seth and me downstairs," she says.

"All right," I say.

After I've gotten dressed in the tight black pants and blue T-shirt Maria left out for me, I head downstairs. Maria and Seth are waiting for me there. "Here," Maria says, handing me a giant and heavy backpack. "This should have just about everything you'll need for your journey."

"Wait," Seth says. "She's not coming with me."

"Why not?" I ask, putting on the backpack.

"Because you'll only slow me down. And didn't you hear what my parents said? If you die, I die. I can't take that chance," Seth says.

I put on the shoes Maria gives me and say, "I'm coming with you because you're going to need help, because you're going to need company and because I need to make up for what my parents have done by helping save everyone. So I'm coming, whether you like it or not."

Seth rolls his eyes at me then turns around and starts to leave. "See you later, Maria, thanks for everything" he calls over his shoulder. I say good-bye to Maria and follow him into the forest, into an adventure.

"You know if you die, I die too. It goes both ways, Seth," I say.

"No offense, but there is a higher chance of you dying than me. I'm both stronger and smarter than you," Seth retorts arrogantly.

"You know, just because you say 'no offense' before you say something mean, it does not mean I will not be offended."

"Fine. Offense intended, I'm both stronger and smarter than you, and hence you are a liability on this journey."

"I really want to slap you right now."

"I'd like to see you try," Seth challenges.

I lift my arm up and go to slap him in the face, but right before my hand makes contact, he catches my wrist and pulls me to the ground. I try to get up, but the backpack is really heavy, so I roll around for a bit like a turtle stuck on its back, trying to get up. All the while Seth is laughing at me. When Seth offers me his hand, I hesitate before taking it. He pulls me onto my feet in one swift movement.

"I warned you," he says, still laughing a little as he starts walking again.

"Why are you wearing a long-sleeved shirt?" I ask.

"So that I can hide the fact that I am a Fire Populous, if I need to," Seth replies.

"So, where are we going now?" I say, trying to change the subject.

Seth sighs and slows down so that I can catch up and walk beside him. "We're going back to the Fire Populous' island."

"Why?" I ask; confused as to why he would want to go back to the place from which we just escaped.

"Last night, I thought about what my parents said. I wondered how it would be possible to be able to wield all of the elements. I finally came up with a theory. Maybe this man has a spell book and was somehow able to use it to master all of the elements. So we are going to sneak back to the island, or at least to where my parents' boat sank, and try to find their spell books. It's a long shot since even if there are answers in there, they're probably destroyed—if not by the fire, then from the water. But it's all we've got."

I giggle. "You said we," I point out teasingly.

Seth lets out a mocking laugh. "Don't get too excited," he says in a dismissive tone.

Still playing around, I shove him with my shoulder. Sadly I only make him stumble a little to the side. Seth shoves me back, and I nearly fall into the woods. I give him a look, but he just laughs and keeps walking through the woods.

Once we get to the shore, we climb into the boat in which we arrived. As Seth pushes off, jumps in and starts rowing us away, I take one last look at the island. Although we were only here for one night, it feels safe to me. As we get farther and farther from it, I feel less and less safe. There's no turning back, though, only moving forward. Hopefully, I'll be able to return someday soon.

I sit in silence, looking out into the horizon as Seth rows. All I see is water, and it reminds me of the day my parents betrayed me. It feels like forever ago—so much has changed since then—but it has only been two days.

I don't want to continue thinking about that horrible day, so to distract myself I say, "Seth?"

"Yes?" he replies.

"Remember right before Maria found your parents' voices?"

"Yeah," he says, not sure where I'm going with this—and probably not wanting to discuss his dead parents since it's such a painful subject.

"You were going to tell me something, some legend," I say, hoping he remembers so that he'll finish telling me the story.

"Oh, right. Well, we know for sure that there are Populous for all four of the elements fire, water, earth and air. But some people say there are Populous for the element of Spirit. It is said that they used to be the primary peacekeepers for all of the elements. Apparently they were very powerful. They could do what we could only dream of doing—they could bring spirits back from the dead. If a loved one died and you were able to find their island and bring the body to them, they could heal the body and bring the spirit back to it." Seth looks at me and continues. "Legend has it that they are still out there somewhere; they just hid themselves because so many people came to them, wanting their loved ones brought back from the dead. Knowing this was wrong and against what nature had originally intended, the Spirit Populous hid themselves, never to be seen again. It's been years since anyone's claimed to see one, so people all assume that they're all dead or never existed at all."

"Wow," I say, intrigued by his story. "Do you think they exist?"

"I don't know, I've never met one, but it wouldn't be that surprising because some people do believe that Spirit is an element. Plus, most legends are based on fact," Seth replies.

CHAPTER 8

After rowing in silence the rest of the way, we come to a spot not too far from the shore. Seth pulls out a bottle filled with some blue liquid and drinks it. When he sees my questioning gaze, he smiles and says, "Maria made it for me. It's supposed to numb my body so that it's all right for me to go into the water for a little while, without it hurting like crazy and killing me—and you, I guess." Seth looks at the water nervously. "Hopefully it works, and I can find those books down there. Well, here goes nothing." Seth drinks the blue liquid, dives gracefully into the water and comes back up seemingly unharmed. "Hand me a flashlight," he says. I hand him a flashlight I find in his backpack. Seth turns on the flashlight, takes a deep breath and dives under, swallowed by the darkness as he goes deeper and deeper. The light fades until I can no longer see anything emitting from his flashlight.

After about 20 uneasy minutes of him diving and coming back up, searching tirelessly for the spell books, he comes up with a big frown on his face. He climbs back into the boat and slouches over, covering his face with his hands.

"You couldn't find the books, could you?" I say.

"No," he says, not bothering to look up at me.

"Does that mean they aren't down there at all?" I ask.

"I don't know."

"Maybe you should keep looking then."

"I can't," Seth replies.

"Why not?"

"Because the potion Maria gave me will only last for about a half hour, at the most."

"Then we should go back and get her to make more," I persist, not wanting to give up just yet.

"We can't."

"Why not?"

"Because magic is forbidden, so no one practices it anymore. Without practice, the Populous grow weak when it comes to using it. Maria could barely make this potion. There's no way she could make another. Besides, she could get caught when she goes and buys more ingredients for the potion. If she gets caught trying to cast a spell, they'll know she has a spell book, and all spell books possessed by an Air Populous were supposed to have been given to the Air Populous Queen," Seth explains.

"Oh." I sigh in discouragement. "So what do we do now?"

"I don't know," Seth admits.

"Yes, you do."

"No, I don't."

"Yes, you do."

"How would you know? Can you suddenly read minds?" Seth asks sarcastically.

"No, but you always know what to do," I say.

"Listen, I don't know for sure, but the books might have been retrieved from the ocean by the Fire Populous after the boat sank. They may have brought the books back to the island."

"See, I told you! You knew what to do next," I say.

"It would be very dangerous, and I don't even know if they definitely have the books on the island."

"But if they do have the books on the island—" I start, but Seth cuts me off.

"They would have them carefully hidden and guarded," he says.

"We have to at least try," I say.

"No."

"Seth, if you won't do it for the Populous, then do it for your parents."

"Fine, but if we die, it's your fault."

"Okay, let's go."

"We have to wait until it's dark," Seth says.

I slump back and cross my arms, pouting. I hate waiting around. I stare out at the horizon, avoiding looking at Seth. On my left is nothing but water and blue sky. Being surrounded by water like this makes me very uneasy. I can almost feel the searing pain the water caused me when they dunked me in the water. If only I still had my necklace.

On my right awaits the Fire Populous island. It's really the last place I want to go. After fleeing to it—and then, later on, from it—I find myself reluctant to return. The idea is nerve-racking. What awaits for me there? Angry parents with an army of Fire Populous at their disposal? If we get caught, we are both dead, and it will be my fault, as Seth said. I am the one who let him out and got us both into this mess. That thought leads me to a question I have avoided asking myself over the past few days. Do I regret letting Seth out? If I could, would I go back in time and stop myself from letting him out of that room? I suppose it would be cowardly to say yes, because had I not let him out, then whoever it is who had Seth's parents killed would have no one to at least try to stop him from doing whatever it is he plans on doing. But a cowardly part of me does wish I could go back to the way things were before all of this transpired, back to when my life was simple and boring. At least in that life I was safe and loved by my parents and friends. Now I have no one but Seth, who does not love me, and being with him is what placed my life on the line and lost me everything else in the first place.

I look over at Seth and think about where I found him. Could I really be such a coward? Would I really lock him back up in a closet because I am afraid? Other than when I first let him out, he's done nothing but comfort me, keep me company and keep me safe and alive. Although he is arrogant, obnoxious and rude, he does not deserve to be locked in that closet. So the answer to my question is no, I would not go back in time so I could make all of this disappear. If I could go back in time, I would do it all again.

I snap back to the present when I feel the boat moving. It is now dark out, and Seth is rowing. We approach the island as quickly and quietly as possible. We need to get on the island, find the books, take them with us and leave the island unnoticed. The consequences of not doing so could be fatal for not only us, but all Populous.

Once we reach the island, we get off the boat, and Seth pulls it in and hides it in the bushes. We run through the trees and to the edge of the village. The village is empty; everyone must be either sleeping or hanging out inside the house.

Seth and I cautiously step out of the brush. I follow Seth as he leads me through the village. I have no idea where we are going; I can't even begin to guess where the spell books are hidden. Seth seems to know where to go, though, so I follow. When we start to return to the forest, I start to wonder where he is taking us, and I doubt that he knows what he is doing. I become more reluctant to move forward with every step. As we travel deeper and deeper into the forest, the light from the moon fades until there is none. "Where are we going?" I whisper to Seth.

Seth shushes me. I sigh and continue to follow him. Finally the trees part, and in the clearing stands a little stone cottage. Seth leads me to the side where there is a lone window. He throws a rock through the window and climbs through, pausing to help me. Once we are both in, Seth turns on a light, which illuminates the interior of the building. From the outside the building looks small, quiet and modest. The brown stones blend in with the forest, making it easy to miss, if you weren't looking for it. On the inside, there are rows upon rows of old looking books and scrolls, placed upon golden painted shelves. It's a giant library, full of secrets waiting to be seen, mysteries waiting to be solved.

"We need to hurry and find the books," Seth says.

"What are we looking for?" I ask.

"Two books were on the boat the night they sank it. They were identical: old with a faded gold cover. They are entitled 'Power: Volume One' and 'Power: Volume Two.'

I search through the shelves, looking for these books. "Do you know what's in them?"

"Pretty much everything you need to know about power—taking it, giving it, stuff like that. If this guy is after power, and I'm guessing he is, these books will contain all we need to know to stop him" Seth says.

"What is this place, by the way?"

"The forbidden archives. All the spell books from the Fire Populous island are in this room."

"So if this place is full of important books, then shouldn't there be an alarm system?" I ask.

"There is."

"What?"

"There's an alarm system," he repeats.

"Then why are you so calm?" I ask, quickening my searching.

"Because panicking will make me miss something," he replies.

We continue our search in silence. "When will the guards come for us?" I ask.

"Soon," is all Seth says.

"All these books look the same! We'll never find it in time!"

"They're here," Seth says.

"The books?" I ask excitedly.

"No, the guards," Seth says, turning to me. "Run and hide in the forest. They'll think it's just me here. Once they leave with me, come back and finish looking. Remember, don't panic or you'll miss something. Once you have the books, get back to the boat and row yourself to the Air Populous island. Maria will take over from there."

"What? No! I won't just leave you here," I argue.

"Listen, if we both run, there's no way we'll be able to get back in here and get those books. If we both get caught, there will be no way to get those books. The only way to get those books is if they catch me, and you come back for them."

"Fine," I say before Seth helps me through the window. I start running for the cover of the forest.

Moments later, a group of Fire Populous emerge from the forest and enter the house. I watch in agony as the guards enter the building and drag Seth out. They are very rough with him, pushing him forward with a knife at his throat. As agreed, I wait until they are gone. When they leave, I jump through the broken window and continue my search for the books. About an hour passes before I've searched the whole place. I look at every book in the library with no success. I sit down on the gold leather couch and stare at the golden table that holds a golden candlestick and little golden bowl. Everything in this room is golden! Even the walls and carpet are golden! I hate it! Gold is too much of a magical colour! Nothing magical has happened in this room! And now Seth is gone, captured by my parents and the Fire Populous. Now I'm all alone. What am I going to do now? What will happen to me—and to Seth? I start to panic. The book has to be here! *Remember, don't panic or you'll miss something.* I remember Seth saying to me. I close my eyes and take a deep breath. When I open my eyes again, I see a statue with marble fire coming out the top. The thing that makes it stand out to me is the fact that it's the only thing in the room that is not golden—it's white. I get up off the couch and walk over to the statue. I study it, not even sure what I'm looking for. I think back to the movies I've seen and books I've read. In those stories, people push the statue over, and a hidden room presents itself. So with lack of a better idea, I give the statue a shove. The statue tilts, and a little trap door opens up behind me. I walk over and climb down the stairs. In the room there are more books. Bigger and older-looking books.

This part of the library is dark and dusty, almost medieval looking. It is a huge contrast to the room above; it is only illuminated by the torches on the wall.

I search the library and find the books a short while later. Once I have the books, I return to the boat and put them in. I pause, remembering Seth's directions to leave him behind, but I can't seem to get myself to do it. I turn around and head back to the village. He's probably not in the jail, since he escaped it before, so he must be in one of the other buildings. I walk through the now-illuminated village, sticking to the shadows. Everyone is out and gathered around in a wide circle. I push my way through the crowd, keeping my head down. When I get near enough to see but not near enough to be seen, I take in the scene in front of me. Seth is there, being held by two guards, one on each side. From his posture, it looks as if the guards at his side are the only things keeping him standing. I cringe at the thought of what they have done to make the proud Seth I know slump to the ground like that.

As the man standing to the left of them speaks to the crowd, I try to think of ways to get both Seth and I out of here alive with the books. It will be a challenge with all these Fire Populous around, especially with Seth looking so weak and beat up. I'm going to need a distraction—something big—but what? I don't have any tools or anything except for my fire power. I look around at the village. I'm going to have to set something on fire, but what? What would be a big enough distraction to clear this giant crowd? Fire doesn't really harm us, but it does knock us down if one uses the right amount of power—sort of like being in an explosion, but less painful and no burns.

I run from the crowd and towards some of the buildings that are farther away. I'm going to have to light the whole place up if I'm going to keep the Populous busy long enough for us to escape. Once I reach a building, I ignite my hand and place it on the wooden door of the house. Once it is in flames and I'm sure it will consume the whole house, I move on to the next. I've lit almost half of the buildings before anyone notices they're engulfed in flames. I quicken my pace and start lighting the fires from the backs of the houses as the Fire Populous start to rush to the flames and absorb the fire. Once I've ignited all the houses around the gathering, I look over to see if I can reach Seth and get him out without too many people trying to stop me. Only half of the crowd is tending to the fires; the other half simply watches them. I need more distractions! I look around, searching for something else to ignite. The forest is the only thing close enough for them to see.

I run to the forest and start setting it on fire. *I'm sorry,* I silently say to the forest. I return to the clearing in a wide half circle and find all of the Fire Populous, except for the two guards holding Seth, running to the forest to put out the quickly spreading fire. Once I get to where they stand, I shoot two fireballs at them and grab Seth as they fly backwards.

Seth leans on me for support as we try to flee the island. Seth is trying to run on his own as much as he can, but he can barely even stand straight, leaving me trying to drag him through the forest. Even with some help, Seth is heavy, and I find myself stumbling a lot—too much, if we plan on making it back to the boat before the whole island is looking for us. I stop for a moment because this isn't working. I prop Seth up on a tree and walk in front of him. I grab his arms and drape them over my shoulders and half piggyback, half drag Seth the rest of the way to the boat.

Once there, I prop Seth up again and pull the boat closer to the water so that the boat is half in, half out. Then I grab Seth, drag him to the boat and help him in. When Seth is safely in the boat, I jump in, grab the paddles, and start rowing. By this time, the Fire Populous have reached the shore and are throwing fireballs at our boat. They miss each time, but the force of the fireballs landing in the water by the boat shakes us, making us almost tip over. The waves splash all over, including on our skin, branding us with agonizingly painful little licks.

As we distance ourselves from the attackers, the ocean quiets, and I allow myself a moment to breathe. Then I continue to row us back to the Air Populous island, not daring to look at Seth for too long. At first glance, he looks like he was beaten almost to death, which I'm sure he was, but if I look closer, then I'll really see the extent of his injuries, and with the Fire Populous possibly grabbing boats to follow us right now, I have no time to freak out and possibly throw up. I have to stay strong and in control of the situation at hand.

As I row, Seth seems to drift in and out of consciousness. When he is conscious, he switches between moaning in pain and mumbling about how stupid I was to go back for him. I ignore him as much as possible. When he is unconscious, his breathing is ragged and laboured, and his body shakes with pain.

The sun is rising when I finally get us to the island. I pull the boat onto shore and run to get Maria to help me with Seth. My legs are stiff from sitting, and my arms burn from rowing. My whole body begs me to lay down and sleep, but I can't—I have to get help for Seth.

When I reach Maria's house, I bang on her door until she answers. Maria stares at me for a moment and rubs her eyes. Her hair is a bit messy, and she wears a light blue night gown and no makeup. Even in this state, she is lovely. In fact she is more beautiful this way, less uptight looking.

When she finishes taking me in, her gentle blue eyes widen in worry. "What's wrong? Where's Seth?" she asks.

Unable to come up with any words, I just motion for her to follow and turn and run towards Seth, not bothering to look back to see if she follows. When I reach the boat, I point towards it. "Seth's hurt. I need your help carrying him in."

Maria approaches the boat and gasps at what she sees. I still don't dare to look at him, not until us and the books are safe inside Maria's house. I start to bend over to pick Seth up when Maria puts a hand on my back, stopping me. "Look out," she says, and she holds her hands out, palms up. She lifts her hands slightly, and a gust of wind lifts Seth up. She starts heading to her house with Seth floating ahead of her on a bed of wind. I pull the boat into the bushes, grab the books and follow.

Once inside, Maria puts Seth in the living room on her couch. She cuts off his shirt with some scissors, and then she starts dressing his wounds and giving him medicine for the pain. I put the books down on her coffee table and help her, now really looking at Seth's injuries as Maria takes care of them. First she has to stitch up a cut on his forehead, which is a horrible experience because he wakes up just as she starts, and he thrashes around and yells. I have to lie on top of him to try to keep him still. After that he passes out again for the rest. Maria then pokes and prods him. If Seth cringes, she wraps up whatever hurts and orders me to get ice, put it in plastic bags and place them on the injury.

Maria ends up wrapping up his right wrist, torso and left shoulder. Once she has done that, she explains her theories on his injuries. She explains she is no doctor, but she believes he has a couple of broken ribs, a sprained wrist and ankle, badly bruised shoulders and shins, some burns from the water, a black eye and a broken nose.

Maria then leaves it to me to clean up as much of his blood as possible. As I am wiping the blood off his face, Seth wakes up again. He does not speak or yell, or even move; he just stares at me as I clean him up. I try to decipher the expression in them but am unable to, for they seem to hold none. There is no anger, pain, gratefulness or fear in his eyes as he stares at me; he just stares.

When I am done, I grab a gray knitted blanket and gently place it on him. Then I leave him to rest and go to the spare bedroom Maria let me use before, to do the same.

The next day, I get up, get dressed and head downstairs to check on Seth. I smile, surprised to see him sitting up and reading one of the spell books. Seth looks up and gives me a half smile before he returns to his reading. My heart races at the sight of it, and at the knowledge that his smile was for me. I walk over and sit down beside him.

As he reads, I can't help but stare at him. *Why am I so attracted to him?* I think to myself. *Why do I feel this connection between us that seems to keep getting stronger every moment I'm with him?*

Seth looks up and stares at me. "What?" I ask, wondering what he is doing, staring at me with a mock confused look on his face.

"Is everything all right? You haven't been going on and on about nothing for a while," he says in a teasing tone.

"Everything is perfectly fine, thank you very much. I was just letting you rest for a while," I say, crossing my arms and looking away from him childishly. Seth laughs at me then continues reading again. "How are you feeling?" I ask.

"Like shit," Seth answers, not bothering to look up from the book.

"Are you hungry for breakfast?"

"Yes." He still doesn't look up.

"Do you want me to get you some?"

"Yes."

"What do you want?" I ask.

"Chef's choice," he says.

I go the kitchen and prepare a gourmet meal: Froot Loops cereal. Then I bring it out to him and make my own. We eat together on the couch in silence. Once we are done, we put our bowls on the coffee table, and I lean back on the couch. Seth picks the book up and says, "Thank you for not leaving me behind." Then he starts reading again.

"You're welcome," I reply with a smile.

Once Seth has had enough of reading, he sits back and crosses his arms across his chest, taking a break. "So Rose," he says, "you unfortunately know plenty about me, but I know next to nothing about you."

"What do you want to know?" I ask.

"Well, first of all, I want to know the truth about you and your many friends," he says.

I sigh. "How did you know I was lying?" I ask him.

He laughs. "First of all, I know I'm charming, funny, smart and not to mention extremely good looking—but I was still a prisoner, and you chose to hang out with me during your spare time, meaning you hadn't made any friends here, meaning you couldn't have been very good at making friends back at your old home."

I roll my eyes and say sarcastically, "You forgot to mention how modest you are. But unfortunately, you're right: I didn't have very many friends. Actually I only had two, Macy and Adam." I avoid his gaze.

"Do you miss them?" he asks.

"Yes, but I'm glad they're not here. I'm glad they're safe and sound at their houses."

Seth continues to stare at me, making me self-conscious and nervous. To try to get him to stop, I ask, "So where are we going now?"

"I don't know," he admits.

"You don't know?"

"Nope," he says, and he grabs the spell books and starts reading them again. I sit there and try to wait patiently while he reads, but as the minutes tick by, it becomes harder and harder to do. I'm just so bored!

"Did you find anything yet?" I ask.

"Yep."

"Then why didn't you tell me?" I ask, annoyed that he made me sit there in silence, bored to death while he pretended to read.

"Because if I told you, then you would have started talking, so I wouldn't have been able to come up with a plan," he says, putting the books down carefully and leaning back.

I sigh. "Did you come up with a plan?"

"Yep."

When he doesn't continue, I ask, "Are you going to tell me what that is?"

"Sure," he says. "On one condition." He shoots me his stupid little smirk that somehow manages to make my heart flutter. Only a little bit, though.

"And what would that be?" I ask, crossing my arms and lifting one questioning brow.

"After I tell you, you have to do me one little favour, no matter what it is," he says.

"What? No way," I say, "For all I know, you could ask me to rub your feet or something."

Seth laughs. "I can assure you it won't be anything like that. Now, do you want to hear my plan or not?"

"Fine," I say.

"Just to clarify. That means you're agreeing to my terms?"

I sigh and say, "Yes, that means I'm agreeing to your terms."

"You promise? No matter what?"

"Yes! Now tell me your plan already, before I come to my senses and change my mind!" I yell, my patience running thin. "I said I agreed, didn't I?"

"Say it," he insists.

"Say what?" I ask, now frustrated.

"Say you promise." He's unfazed by my tone of voice.

My voice becomes gentler. "I promise," I say.

"All right. In the books it says that the only way to be able to control more than one of the elements is to kill a Populous from the element you want to be able to wield, and cast a certain spell—which is in the book—after you've killed them. For the spell to work, you need to use the dead Populous' blood, but it only works if the Populous is actually dead." Seth pauses, looking at me as if to make sure I can handle what he just said. When I stare at him, he continues. "It also says that the only way to destroy a person who can wield more than one element would be to use the elements he can wield against him and absorb the power out of him. For example, this guy can apparently wield all four of the elements, so for us to destroy him, we would have to use all four of the elements against him." He pauses again, making sure I'm still paying attention. "So what I'm getting at is, either we have to kill one Populous from the three of the four elements we don't wield, or we recruit one Populous from the three elements we don't wield."

"Well, I think it's safe to say we'll be recruiting some Populous," I say.

"Yep, but we'll have to make sure we pick strong Populous, because if we're going to absorb the power from whoever this guy is, I'm assuming we'll have to be pretty strong."

"Yeah, okay, so where to?" I ask.

"I'm not done explaining what we need to do," Seth says.

"Sorry. Please continue," I say, rolling my eyes at him again.

"Once the powers have been absorbed from him, to kill him for good and to free the spirits of the Populous from whom he stole the powers from, we must slit his throat with the Cinquedea des Morts."

"What's that?" I ask.

"A Cinquedea is a type of dagger, and 'des Morts' means of the dead."

"And where do we find this dagger of the dead?"

"It doesn't say," Seth says.

"So what are we supposed to do?" I ask.

"Maybe Maria knows," Seth suggests.

"Well, it's worth a shot." I say. When Seth doesn't get up and continues to lounge on the couch, I ask, "Are we going to ask Maria or what?"

"I don't know about you, but I'm going to sleep," he says lounging farther back in the couch. "I sort of got beat almost to death yesterday. I need my beauty sleep."

I sigh in exasperation and watch him close his eyes—which were already half closed from the bruising—and fall asleep. I grab the remote off the coffee table and flip through the channels. I have no desire to do much of anything today; I was the one who dragged Seth to safety last night, and I think I deserve a break, too.

Seth sleeps for most of the day, only waking up for meals and to go to the bathroom. Maria and I take turns bringing him his meals. That's a breeze. It's the bathroom breaks that take a lot out of us and Seth. When he has to go, Maria and I both help him walk to the bathroom, but he refuses to let us hold him up while he goes, so by the time we help him back to the couch, he passes out and sleeps until the next meal or bathroom break.

"When will he start feeling better?" I ask Maria two days later.

"I think if we wait for him to heal naturally, it will take too long. That's why I went to the store and bought some healing ingredients."

"Why haven't you made the potion yet? Is there something you need help with?" I ask.

"No, it's just that the only healing potion recipe I have can only be made when the moon is full," Maria replies.

"When is that?"

"Tonight."

That night, Maria goes to her room to make the spell while I watch Seth. Seth seems pretty relaxed and pain-free at the moment, but I know as soon as he stands, he won't feel that way. I sit down beside him on the couch and pull some of his blankets on my lap. "How are you feeling?" I ask him.

"Fine," he says, not bothering to look away from the TV. He's watching some action movie where things blow up every two seconds.

"Maria is making you a healing potion to speed up your recovery."

"That's nice." He's been like this for the last three days: quiet, polite and tired, very tired. I almost miss his snarky, arrogant comments. This Seth worries me; it isn't even Seth, or at least not the one I know. I'm hoping the healing potion will fix this, too.

Maria walks in with the healing potion and hands it to Seth, who takes it and drinks it. Maria and I both watch as he gulps it down. When Seth is done, he hands Maria the empty glass and returns to his TV watching.

"The potion should make you feel and look a lot better tomorrow," Maria says, and then she leaves.

I stay with Seth and watch the rest of his movie with him. When that movie is over, another one starts, and we are both fast asleep halfway through the movie.

CHAPTER 9

The next morning, I wake up on the couch with Seth right beside me. During the night, we must have lied down side by side on the couch. Seeing him with his face so close to my face, his lips so close to my lips . . . I bolt up and away from him, not liking the felling of rightness I felt at having him so close to me.

Seth wakes up as the couch groans from my sudden movement. He sits up beside me. "Morning," he mumbles.

"Good morning," I say back. I must admit, I was caught a little off guard by his niceness. "How are you feeling?"

"A lot better, actually."

"You look better," I say, and I mean it. His black eye is gone, and the scratches and bruises on the rest of his body are, too.

Maria comes down from her room and inspects Seth. She takes off all of his bandages and gets him to stand, walk and jump around a bit. He passes all of her tests, and she deems him healed.

"Did you find anything when you went through the books a few days ago?" Maria asks.

"Sort of," Seth says. "Do you happen to know anything about the Cinquedea des Morts?"

"As a matter of fact, I do. My father had a fascination with weapons, especially the older types. He had this book full of them. It's also known as the Dagger of the Dead."

"Well, we need it, but we don't know where we can get our hands on one," Seth says.

"I'll see if I can find my father's book," Maria says, leading us through her house to her bedroom. She tells us to wait by the door and then grabs a giant, old, brown leather-bound book.

We follow her to the living room, where we all sit down on the couch, Maria in between Seth and me. Maria opens the book and skims through the pages until she finds one titled "Cinquedea des Morts." We all read the page.

"It says that the Cinquedea des Morts somehow ended up in a human museum in Paris, called La Musée des Armes."

"We'll have to go to Paris and break into the museum and get it," Seth says.

"What? We're going to break into a museum?" I exclaim.

"You don't have to come."

"I'm coming, but it's just . . . there are humans, and breaking in and stealing a relic seems wrong."

"That's because it *is* wrong," Seth says. "But it's necessary."

Maria sighs. "Ah, Paris, the city of love." We both look at Maria. "What? It is," she says defensively.

"We'll leave first thing tomorrow," Seth says.

That day, we hang out with Maria, prepare for tomorrow and then go to bed. When I wake up, I put on the human-style clothes waiting for me on the dresser and then go downstairs, where Seth and Maria are talking. We eat breakfast, grab our bags and head out. "Bye, Maria, see you soon," Seth and I say as we are leaving.

Seth and I get into the boat, and Seth rows us to the dock where the boat that brought me to this adventure used to be. We dock the boat, grab our bags and walk to the nearest airport. Once we get to the airport, Seth buys our tickets. (I'm not sure where he got the money.) Then we sit down and wait for our flight, which won't depart for three hours.

To try to pass the time, I talk to Seth. "Have you ever been to Paris?"

"No," he says.

"Where did you get the money to pay for the tickets?"

"Maria gave it to me."

"Are you going to pay her back?"

"Yes."

"Are you excited to go to Paris?"

"Not really."

"Why not?"

"Because I'm only going to steal a dagger."

"Are you angry I'm coming?" I ask hesitantly.

"No. Why do you ask?"

"Because, you aren't conversing with me."

"I'm answering all of your questions, aren't I?"

"Yeah, with as few words as possible."

"Sorry, I'm just thinking."

"About what?"

"What the next step will be."

"Have you come up with anything?"

"Not yet," he says.

We sit in silence for a while, and I let Seth think. Eventually, though, I can't take it anymore. "Did it hurt, getting your tattoo?"

"Not really, but I'm a lot tougher than you, so it might hurt you when you get yours," he replies.

"I'll have to get one?" I ask nervously.

"If you decide to stay on the island after all of this, then yes. It tells other Populous what type of Populous you are."

"Can I get a closer look at yours?" I ask, wanting to see exactly what I may have to get permanently inked onto my skin.

"Sure," Seth says, holding his left arm out in front of me.

I hold his arm in my hands and feel a current run through me. I shiver and feel him do the same. I shake my head to clear it and inspect the tattoo. It pretty much looks the same up close as it does faraway. I start to twist his arm to get a look at the back, when he pulls him arm away, laughing. "What are you trying to do, twist my arm off?"

"Sorry," I say.

Three hours later, after small talk and Seth teasing and mocking me, we finally board the plane. I've been on a plane only once in my life, and I was little, so I don't really remember much. I only remember the destination: Disney World. I had a wonderful time there and remember crying when it was time to go home.

I am brought back to reality when Seth nudges me forward and says, "We're in seats 10 and 11." I find the seats, and we sit down by the window. Seth sits down beside me, and later we are joined by an old man who smells bad. He is sitting in the aisle seat beside Seth.

I watch as everyone finds her or his seat and jump when I hear a loud noise behind me. I twist around in my seat and see a man helping a woman with her carry-on. He looks normal at first, but then I see the hint of a Fire Populous tattoo peeking out from under his sleeve as he puts the woman's bag in the carry on compartment above the seats. I quickly turn around and tell Seth about what I just saw.

"It could just be someone with a fire tattoo on their arm, but if it is a Fire Populous, then you have nothing to worry about while we're on the plane with all of these humans and we'll be extra careful once we get off, alright?" Seth says.

"Alright," I say.

Once everyone is seated, the flight attendant goes over safety regulations and what to do in an emergency. When she finishes, the plane starts to roll up the runway. I quickly buckle up and pull the belt as tight as it can go.

"What's wrong?" Seth asks. "You seem really tense. Are you still worried about that man?"

"I'm a little nervous about flying," I say. "What if we crash?"

"We won't crash," Seth says, laughing.

"It's not funny; planes have crashed before, you know."

"You'll be fine, trust me."

"Trust you? Ha!"

"In case you haven't noticed, you've been trusting me with your life this whole time," he says.

"How?" I ask.

"By just being here with me."

The plane starts taking off, and I brace myself. We go higher and higher, and my ears start to pop. I look out the window and see the ground becoming more distant; the things still on the ground becoming smaller and smaller. I tighten my seat belt even more. I barely acknowledge Seth removing my hands from the seat belt and loosening it a bit; I just can't seem to tear my eyes away from the window. I am solely focused on how high we are getting.

"How much higher do you think we'll go?" I ask Seth.

"Lots higher. We just took off, Rose."

I take hold of my seat belt and start tightening it again. Seth removes my hands and loosens the seat belt yet again, but this time he takes my hands in his. When I try to pull my hands away to place them on my seat belt, he won't let go. His grip is gentle yet strong enough to keep me from cutting off the circulation from my waist down with the seat belt.

We stay like that until the plane levels out and stops climbing higher. Then he cautiously lets go, making sure that my hands won't return to my seat belt. When they don't, he relaxes back in his seat. I try to do the same, but I can't stop looking out the window and thinking about how high up we are, so I close the blinds.

"How long do you think this flight will be?" I ask.

"It's going to be about five hours," Seth replies.

"Five hours?" I gasp.

"Why don't you try to sleep or watch some TV?" he suggests.

"Okay." I lie back and close my eyes. I alternate between sleeping, watching TV and freaking out. Seth mostly sits quietly, watching TV, sleeping or calming me down.

When we finally land, I hurry off the plane. I wait for Seth to catch up, and then we go and get our bags. We haven't packed very big bags because we won't be staying long. We just packed the necessities, all of which were given to us by Maria.

Once we have our bags, we hail a taxi, which brings us to our hotel, always making sure we are not being followed.

Chapter 10

Our hotel is quite nice. It's big and tall, and everything is spotless on the inside of the glorious lobby. It is actually quite fancy, with the crystal chandelier, red velvet loveseats and a grand piano taking up the space the front desk does not.

We check in and head upstairs to our room. When we enter our room, I see two beds with beige bedspreads and brown wooden bed frames. There are a bunch of white and beige pillows on the head of the bed. The floors are white carpet and the walls are dark brown, giving off a dimming effect in the room. There is a TV, a dark brown dresser, a dark brown side table in between the beds, and a glass table and wooden chairs by the window for us to eat at. The bathroom is on the other side of the room, and so is the closet. The windows are covered by dark brown velvet drapes.

"Wow, this place is nice," I say, picking the bed closest to the window and table and placing my bag on it.

Seth places his bag on the other bed and hands me a key card. "Yeah, it's really fancy."

"So when are we going to . . . you know . . ."

"Rob the museum?" Seth says like it's no big deal.

"Yeah."

"Well, I was thinking we would relax for the day, come up with a plan in the evening and then get the dagger later tonight, after the museum is closed, which would be around 10."

I look at the clock. We had left at eight in the morning, and it is now one in the afternoon. "All right," I say.

Seth turns towards the door and starts to leave. "Where are you going?" I ask.

"I am going to get something to eat," Seth replies.

"Do you mind if I join you?" I ask.

"No."

"No, you don't mind, or no, I can't join you?"

"You pick," Seth says, turning to face me so I can see his signature smirk lighting up his face. I give him a playful shove and follow him out the door.

We head to the hotel's restaurant, which is much like the rest of the hotel: very fancy. The tables and chairs are all dark brown wood. The chairs have a red velvet cushion that matches the drapes, which keep the outside light from coming in and ruining the ambiance of the room. The tables have red velvet place mats on them. The walls are beige, the floors are dark wood, and the lights are dimmed. There are a few other people occupying some of the tables.

A waitress comes and greets us. I immediately notice the extra nice smile this pretty, voluptuous, blonde waitress flashes Seth. I also notice the hostile look she gives me, as if I have no right to be dinning with him. I'm not sure why, but I hook my arm through Seth's and smile sarcastically at her for good measure.

The waitress grudgingly takes us to a table by the windows—or should I say the giant, red drapes. "Est-ce que je peut vous commencer avec quelque chose à boire?" She asks us in a too perky voice, once we are seated.

"Um, do you speak English?" Seth asks her.

"Oui, yes. Can I start you two off with something to drink?" she says.

"Yeah, I'll have an iced tea, please," Seth says.

"Sure thing!" the waitress says.

"I'll have the same," I say. I don't get an answer from her; she just writes it down and then leaves.

"What was that all about?" Seth asks.

"Um, I don't really know," I say. "I think she likes you."

"You think so?" Seth asks.

"Yeah."

"Is that why you put your arm through mine back there, so that she knew I was off-limits?" Seth says, smirking.

"No!" I say too quickly. "And you're not off-limits. Who said you were off-limits?"

Seth laughs. "All right, in that case maybe I'll ask her for her number. She *is* cute and has a nice accent."

"You can do whatever you want," I say with a huff.

"Okay then, I will," Seth says, still smirking.

When the waitress comes back with our drinks, we order our food. I order pasta, and he orders chicken wings.

"It must be nice, eating real food again," I blurt out before I can stop myself.

"Yeah, it is. It's nice to be able to do a lot of things again. I see everything differently now. It's hard to truly appreciate something—or someone, for that matter—until you lose it. You know that saying: you don't know what you've got until it's gone?"

"Yeah."

Seth says, "Well, it is a very true saying, and I definitely know what I've got now, whereas before I didn't."

"Wow," I joke, "who knew you could be that deep."

Seth laughs. "I'm being serious."

"What were you like when you were growing up?" I ask.

"Well, let me see . . . I was just as amazing as I am now, and I looked pretty much like I do now, only now I look better."

"I'm being serious," I say, imitating what he had said to me before.

"So am I," he says. "I'm better looking than I used to be when I was younger. I'm taller and more muscular, and my features are more grownup, more manly."

I sigh. "Seriously, what was it like for you growing up?"

Seth pauses and says, "Well, if you must know . . . like I said, I was a total stud, but I was terribly shy."

"You? Shy?" I exclaim, interrupting him.

"Hey! Do you want to hear about my childhood or not?"

"Sorry."

"Then shut up and let me tell you!" Seth says.

I am about to give him crap for telling me to shut up, when the waitress comes with our food. "Here you go," she says, placing our food down in front of us. "Bon appétit." She is only addressing Seth.

"Thank you," Seth says sweetly, and he takes her hand and kisses it while looking directly at me with a smirk on his face.

When the waitress all but swoons before walking away, I shake my head at him. "That was pathetic," I say.

"Whatever do you mean?" Seth says with a fake innocent look plastered on his face.

"Did you see her? She practically fainted. You shouldn't tease her like that—it's not nice."

"It's completely harmless," Seth says.

"Okay." I say in a non-committal tone. "So can you finish telling me about your childhood?"

"Sure, but then you have to tell me about yours," Seth replies.

"Deal."

"I was born March 18, and that makes me a Pisces. My mother's name was Lily, and my father's name was Anthony. I was born on the Fire Populous' island. I am an only child and never had any pets. When I was a child, all of the Populous were closer allies, almost friends, and so I became friends with Keith and Maria. I mostly hung out with Keith because Maria was less adventurous back then, and Keith and I liked to go on adventures—or at least, that's what we called them. Our parents called it trouble."

I laugh, picturing Seth and another little boy getting into all kinds of trouble. He continues. "But over the years, the Populous became more distant and more distinguished. I'm guessing it was from the brainwashing pills we were taking. My childhood gradually got worse. At first I was just a normal kid with friends and a family. Then I slowly lost my friends because they were a different kind of Populous, and the different kinds of Populous couldn't seem to live in peace anymore. We started traveling and investigating the Fire Demons, and I lost my family. Then I lost the only thing I had left: my freedom." Seth pauses to look at me, "And that is the wonderful life of Seth Harris."

"Wow, I always seem to forget how tough your childhood was," I say, still eating my pasta.

"I told you my story. It's your turn," Seth says, continuing with his food.

"Well, I was born October 18. That would make me a Libra."

Seth laughs. "Hmm, I wonder if we're compatible."

I give him a glare and continue. "My mother's name is Gwen, and my father's name is Paul. I grew up with friends and a family. Unlike you, I was a good girl: I got good grades and stayed out of trouble. My life was a perfectly normal one, which I found very boring—that is, until I opened that door and let you out. Then I was rushed to an island, told that I am not human, shown how to wield fire and dunked in an ocean by my parents. Then I had to run away from them, and now here I am, eating dinner before stealing a knife from a museum, so that we can kill the person who has been trying to control us all for some unknown reason. And that is the wonderful life of Rosalie Evers."

"Well, I guess it's safe to say we're probably both really screwed up from all that has happened to us," Seth says.

"Yep, pretty much."

We pay once we're done eating, and Seth says good-bye to the waitress, who practically cries because she is so upset. Then we return to our room.

When we enter, I look at the clock: six thirty. We have roughly four hours before we go rob a museum.

Seth grabs the TV remote and plops down on his bed, turning the TV on. Before he can start flipping through the channels, I ask "You know how to work a TV?"

Seth gives me an incredulous look. "You're kidding, right?" he asks.

"Well, you have been locked in a room for some time . . ."

Seth laughs. "When do you think they invented TVs? Right after I was locked up?"

"Well, I guess if you put it that way . . . But there is also the fact that you did live on the Fire Populous island before that." I say.

"Just because I lived on an island doesn't mean I didn't watch TV. I admit I didn't watch much, but I do know how to work a remote, Rose."

"Sorry." I sit down on my bed quietly before I say something else stupid.

Seth flips through the channels until he finds some beauty pageant. It's in French, but Seth probably isn't interested in what they're saying. "Change it," I order.

"No."

"Seth, this is totally inappropriate."

"How?"

"These girls are in bikinis!"

"Exactly," Seth says with a grin.

I pounce on his bed and snatch the remote from him. "I am *not* watching this." I say, and I change the channel to a French soap opera.

"I am not watching *that*!" Seth says, and he tries to regain control of the remote.

"I don't think so!" I jump off the bed and out of his reach. Seth gets off the bed and walks towards me. I jump onto my bed and stand on the side farthest away from him, with the remote far out of his reach. I turn the volume up, and the crying of a broken-hearted woman becomes louder. Seth pounces onto the bed, and I jump off, barely escaping. I run to his bed and jump on it. Seth slowly approaches to bed, barely able to hide his grin. I wave the remote above my head and stick my tongue out at him, taunting him.

"That's it," Seth says, and he grabs the quilt off the bed and pulls it out from under me, making me fall on the bed. Before I can push myself up, Seth jumps on the bed and lies down on his stomach beside me, grabbing the remote from my hands. Seth rolls over, but before he can push himself up, I'm on him. Seth puts his arm above his head, keeping the remote just out of my reach. Laughing, I try to inch my way up so I can reach the remote. Seth changes the channel back to the beauty pageant and drops the remote on the floor. I try to push myself up and off of him so I can get it, but Seth won't let me. He rolls over so that he is on top of me, and he turns his head and starts watching TV as I struggle underneath him. Suddenly I am aware of his closeness. I can feel the heat emanating from his body; his heartbeat is racing from chasing me.

Suddenly Seth looks at me as if he can feel it, too—feel my heat and my heart racing not only from running from him but from his closeness. His face is now even closer to mine because he is looking down at me. For a moment we just stare at each other as if memorizing each other's faces. I feel Seth hands slowly moving to my waist. My breath starts coming faster as I anticipate the feel of his hands moving to my legs, but instead he puts his hands on the bed and pushes himself off of me. I sit up and straighten my hair out.

"You can change it now, if you want. I'm going to go for a walk," Seth says, heading for the door. I sit there and stare at him as he leaves. Once he's gone, I change the channel and lie back down. I don't even really acknowledge the TV; it's not like I can even understand what they are saying. I lay there and think about what just happened.

CHAPTER 11

Seth doesn't return until nine o'clock. When he comes through the door, I get up and walk over to him. "Where were you?" I ask.

"I told you I was going for a walk," he replies, unfazed by my accusing tone.

"For that long?"

"Yes. Is that a problem?" Seth asks, becoming more frustrated with me.

"Yes, it is. You left me here for, like, two hours!" I say, raising my voice a little. "I thought you were dead or something! Or worse."

"What could be worse than me being dead?" Seth asks.

"You could have robbed the museum without me!" I say.

Seth laughs and then lounges on his bed. "Wake me up in half an hour," he says before he closes his eyes.

"Whatever." I lie down on my bed and continue to watch the TV shows that I don't understand. After a half hour of that, I wake Seth up, and he gets up and we head out.

"Don't we need supplies or something?" I ask Seth.

"All we need are these," Seth says, pulling out a pair of black ski masks and handing me one.

I stare at the ski mask, thinking of all of the crime movies I've seen where the criminals wore them. The criminals always got caught in those movies . . .

When we reach the museum, it is ten thirty. Even though it is still pretty early, the parking lot is empty except for one car: the night guard's car. The museum is small but elegant and a little eerie in the dark of the night. Seth leads me around back, to the garden. "Why are we back here?" I ask.

"I think we should wait a little bit longer before we do this. We got here sooner than I thought we would."

I spot a bench and sit down. I look around at the roses and rose blossom trees that hide us. Seth joins me on the bench and hands me a red rose. "A lovely rose for my lovely Rose," he says, laughing.

"Ha ha." I look at the rose in my hands and twirl it between my fingers. There are no thorns on this rose, so I don't have to worry about pricking my fingers on it. Seth's words echo in my mind. *A lovely rose for my lovely Rose.* Although he may have meant it as a joke, I can't help blushing. *He thinks I'm lovely,* I think to myself.

I am brought back to the present when I see Seth rest his arm on the back of the bench behind me. I am suddenly very aware of his closeness and of the scenery we have found ourselves in: one girl and one guy, sitting alone together on a bench in a rose garden at night, hidden from peering eyes by the trees. Then I remember how we found ourselves here. We are here to steal from a museum!

Half an hour later, Seth gets up and holds out his hand to help me up. I take it and get up. "Time to rob a museum," Seth says. Even in the dark, I can see him smirking.

I follow Seth to the back of the museum. There is a big window that overlooks the garden. At a corner of the window, Seth places his finger onto the glass. He lights his finger on fire and traces out a square. Then Seth pushes on the glass and catches the square he cut out before it can hit the ground and shatter. He walks into the museum and carefully places the square of glass against the wall. "That was pretty cool," I whisper.

Seth smirks at me in response and then puts on his mask. I place the rose in the side of my pants with the top flower part sticking out, and then I put on my mask. I follow Seth as he walks to where the dagger is. When he finds it, he turns to face me and whispers, "When I cut the glass, the glass will fall into the case and set off the alarm, so we're going to have to make a run for it, okay?"

I nod my head. Seth cuts the glass, and just like he said, the alarm goes off. Seth grabs the dagger and starts running, with me following closely behind. We run a good five blocks before we stop and take off our masks. As we walk back to the hotel, I am constantly looking over my shoulder, keeping an eye out for both the police and the Fire Populous.

"Calm down," Seth says.

"Calm down? We just finished robbing a museum, and you want me to calm down?" I ask, bewildered. "We have giant targets on our backs, and you want me to calm down? We could get killed, and you want me to calm down?"

"I'm sorry, you're right. I forgot about the Fire Populous being after us. I should have guessed they would know that we would try to find the dagger," Seth says.

I say nothing and continue walking and looking around, keeping an eye out for any sign of danger. The moon is our only source of light on this dark street. All of the houses are dark; everyone inside asleep, oblivious to the fact that we robbed a museum and are now walking down the street.

My mind starts to wander, and I imagine the lives of those people: so simple and ordinary. Surprisingly, I don't find myself wishing I could go back home where everything would be normal again. However, I can't help but wonder what my life would have been like if none of this had ever happened, if I hadn't let Seth out. Would I have been happy? Would I have fallen in love? Would I have travelled the world? Who knows?

All of a sudden I hear footsteps on the pavement behind us. I can tell that Seth hears it too, because he puts his arm around my back, and I can feel that the muscles in his arm are tight. "Just keep walking," he whispers to me.

I do as he says. We keep walking, but Seth is not leading us in the direction of our hotel. He is leading us into the little forest ahead.

"What are you doing?" I ask him in a quiet voice.

"Seeing if they follow us into the forest," Seth says.

"How many do you think there are?"

"I don't know. Maybe six or seven."

"If they are Fire Populous, do you think you can take them all on?" I ask Seth nervously.

"Maybe." Seth says.

"That's reassuring," I say sarcastically.

We enter the forest, and the people behind us continue to follow us as we walk on the little gravel path. When Seth turns and leads us off the path, they still follow. Seth suddenly stops, turns around and lowers his hand from my back. The place where his hand was now feels cold without the warmth of his strong hand. I slowly turn around to see who is following us.

Because of the trees of the forest, the light from the moon barely makes it past the leaves, leaving it nearly impossible to see the faces of our followers. I also can't see whether they have tattoos because they are wearing long-sleeved shirts. All I can make out is their silhouettes. Seth and I stand there facing them, waiting for them to make the first move.

Seconds tick by as we continue to stare the followers down. The forest is so silent that I can hear my own heart beating. Finally, one of the seven people who were following us lights his hands on fire in one swift motion. We now know for sure that these are Fire Populous, probably sent here to kill us.

Seth makes the same motion with his hands, and they ignite immediately. The other three followers ignite their hands as well. Feeling I should at least try to do the same, I make the same motion with my hands and pray they light. When they don't, I feel panic and defeat.

One of the followers steps forward and crouches, getting ready to pounce; the others do the same. All at once they start to form fireballs in their hands. Seth swears and takes a step back. "Run and follow me, if you lose me, get to the hotel—make sure they don't follow you," Seth says, and he turns and runs away.

I turn and do the same. I run as fast as I possibly can without stumbling over the tree roots and getting caught in the bushes. *Just follow Seth, just follow Seth,* I think to myself as I run for my life.

Seth twists and turns through the forest; occasionally checking to make sure I am behind him. I turn to glance behind me, to see how close our followers are. They are not far behind; if I were to stumble, they would get me. I turn back around and see that Seth is gone. "Seth!" I call out desperately, but no answer comes. I continue to run, but now I am looking for the path and no longer following Seth. I feel so scared and alone without his presence. *Get to the path, get to the path . . .* I feel the path beneath my feet before I see it. It is so dark. Behind me I hear the footsteps of my followers as their feet hit the pavement of the path.

I finally exit the forest and run down the sidewalk. Oh how I wish I was safe and sound in my bed. I feel my legs start to tire. *Keep running, you have to keep running,* I repeat over and over in my head. I pass house after house, never daring to look behind me. I am now huffing and puffing, using every ounce of strength that I have to keep running at the same pace. I turn a corner and then turn again. I am now behind the houses I just ran past. I am pretty sure the hotel is in this direction. I am running right beside the houses. I know my followers will be turning the corner at any moment. I also know that I have to keep running. What I don't know is how I am going to lose them.

All of a sudden, an arm wraps around my waist, and another covers my mouth, muting my scream. The arms pull me in between two houses and pull me down to a sitting position. I struggle, trying to break free, but the arms only tighten around me. "Rose, it's me," Seth says. At the sound of his voice, I immediately stop struggling and jump into his arms. Seth sits up with me cradled in his lap as we sit quietly and watch our followers run past us. We both let out a sigh of relief. "Are you all right?" he asks.

I take a few seconds to answer as I catch my breath. "Yeah."

Seth lets go of me and I get up. Seth stands, and we start walking back to the hotel.

When we get back into our room, Seth puts the dagger in his suitcase. "Our plane leaves first thing tomorrow," he says. "Hopefully we'll be able to get through security."

Seth lays down in his bed and goes to sleep. I lie down on my bed. It takes only seconds for me to fall asleep after the exhausting events of tonight.

Seth wakes me up the next morning at five o'clock. We both quickly get ready, and then Seth checks out of the hotel. We take a taxi to the airport. When we get to the airport, Seth walks in and heads to one of the little stores in the airport. He buys a little suitcase to put the dagger in. Seth also puts some of the few things he brought into the suitcase. Seth puts the bags on the conveyer belt and watches to make sure it goes through. When it does, they both go through security and board the plane by six thirty.

The plane takes off, and I freak out again. Seth has to work even harder to keep me calm, because my nerves are frayed from robbing the museum and the close call with the Fire Populous. Seth suggests I watch some TV. I turn on the screen and see the museum we just robbed surrounded by cop cars. I quickly turn the TV off. It takes a good 10 minutes before Seth is able to calm me down. When he finally does, I decide to try to sleep for a while. I manage to sleep for about two hours before I wake up. "Dang it," I say.

"What?" Seth asks.

"I have to go to the bathroom."

"So what? Just go."

"I don't want to." I say.

"Why not?" Seth asks.

"Because we're thousands of feet in the air!" I exclaim.

Seth rolls his eyes. "Then hold it," he says.

"For three hours?"

"If you can't hold it, then get up and go. It's not going to kill you."

"How do you know?"

"Just go, Rose!"

"Fine!" I say, getting up slowly. I walk into the bathroom. When done, I flush, wash my hands and practically run back to my seat.

"See, you are perfectly fine," Seth says when I take my seat.

"No, I'm not," I say, huffing and puffing. "I'm scarred for life."

Seth laughs and then sits back and closes his eyes.

Once we land, we grab our bags and take a taxi to a nearby marina and rent a boat. From there Seth drives the boat out to sea.

"Where are we going?" I ask. "Back to the Air Populous island?"

"No, we'll start with trying to recruit an Earth Populous; hopefully we'll be able to find my friend Keith," he says, "Then we'll make our way to the Water Populous' island. They'll probably be a bit harder to convince. After that, we'll circle back to the Air Populous' island and get Maria to help us."

"Are they going to be strong enough?" I ask.

"Yes," Seth says.

"And I'm guessing you're going to be our Fire power?" I ask, half joking—but also hoping that's the plan, because there is no way I'd be able to do it.

"Yep."

He continues to row. As he drives I fill the silence by talking, as usual. This time, though, I find it's more because I'm uncomfortable with the silence—too much time to think. I find now that if I don't keep myself distracted, I either think of my parent's betrayal or my constant confusion and frustration towards Seth. Neither is good.

"Hey, I see the island!" I say. I turn back and look at Seth rowing. Never slowing down, strong muscles always working . . . I blink and shake my head, trying to clear those thoughts.

Once we get to shore, I grab my backpack and get out. Seth follows and brings the boat further in so that it doesn't float away.

"Wow," I say, looking in awe at the jungle in front of me "And I thought the Fire and Air Populous' island was beautiful. They don't even begin to compare to this jungle."

All of its plants and flowers look so alive. It's like they could get up and move on their own at any moment. They dance gracefully in the wind, as if the only thing keeping them from twirling and doing sautés and pirouettes is the lush ground beneath them.

"They are the Earth Populous, after all," Seth says in a tone that suggests that I should already know this. I roll my eyes at him. He smirks at me and starts walking into the jungle. "Stay close." He grabs my arm and pulls me so close to him that I'm basically glued to his back. Being this close to him and feeling his hand around my wrist sends a shiver through me. I can only hope he doesn't feel it.

As we continue to walk through the jungle, I try my best not to step on his heels. "Why do we have to walk so close together?"

"Because we can't disturb the earth, or they'll sense it and know we're here. Then they'll immediately think we're a threat and come and take care of it. And by take care of it, I mean capture us and maybe even kill us."

"I still don't understand why I have to walk so close to you. I can just walk where you walk," I say.

"Fine," he says as he lets go of my wrist. "If you want to take that risk, go ahead. Just stay close and follow my steps exactly."

We continue to walk, and this time I'm not worrying about tripping us both up by stepping on his heels. Even though I can now walk much easier, admittedly, I miss his closeness.

After a little while, I start to slow down a bit to look at all of the beautiful plants. The colours and life are so amazing, so mesmerizing. There are no animals around, though.

"Why are there no animals?" I ask Seth.

"Because the perimeter of the island is a huge alarm system. The animals are farther in."

I'm brought back to high alert when all of a sudden I feel the earth starting to shake beneath us. Seth and I immediately stop where we are.

Seth slowly turns around and comes to where I stand frozen. He gently moves me back a step. Then he looks down at the ground, looks up at me, rolls his eyes and swears. I look down and see a tiny plant, now crushed. It is my turn to swear now. "Seth, I'm so sorry," I say. "I swear I didn't see it."

"I thought I told you to follow *exactly* where I step," Seth says, clearly frustrated by what I've done.

"What do we do now?" I ask.

"There's nothing we can do. They've sensed that the perimeter has been disturbed, and now they're coming for us."

The ground continues to shake more and more until the earth starts to rise up, higher and higher, becoming giant walls that surround us. The walls of earth are too high for us to climb out and too strong for us to break through.

"Who goes there?" a deep voice asks, seeming to come from above us.

I look up and see a man perched on top of one of the walls of earth. "Seth and Rose, two Fire Populous'. We just want to talk," Seth says.

The man looks down at us and asks, "Are you alone?"

"Yes, it's just us," Seth replies.

The man nods, and the walls start to lower, returning to the earth from where they came until they are gone. It looks as if nothing ever happened.

"We would like to speak to your Queen, please," Seth says.

"Follow me," the man says, leading us deeper into their jungle—which, as they have just demonstrated, is also their weapon.

We follow the man as he leads us to his Queen. I'm careful not to step on any other plants. I sure don't want to upset this man or any of the other Earth Populous any more than I already have. Especially not this big, strong-looking man, who towers above Seth's six feet easily.

We reach a clearing, and there's a building that looks to be made purely of vines, plants and other natural materials. The shape of the building is a giant dome. Surrounding it are houses in the trees—giant tree houses.

The man leads us into the giant dome and brings us to what looks to be a throne room. Sitting on the throne is a woman, and a beautiful one at that. She has dark, tan skin and long, black, curly hair. Her attire is solely green. Her skirt is made out of green fabric, which parts in the middle showing off some of her legs. Her top is made of the same material; it covers her chest and leaves her stomach bare. She wears no shoes. Her arms, legs, stomach and face bear green, intricate tattoos that she wears elegantly and fiercely.

As we get closer, I see her eyes. They are so mesmerizing, the most beautiful emerald green I've ever seen. They remind me of Adam's, which reminds me of Macy, which reminds me of the fact that I may never see them again.

She looks at us carefully, measuring us up. When we say nothing, she says, "Well? What are you waiting for? State your business."

Seth clears his throat. "I am Seth, and this is Rose. We are Fire Populous', and we have come to seek your help."

The woman laughs. "You, a Fire Populous, has come to seek our help? May I ask why?"

"We have reason to believe that there is an evil man going from Populous to Populous, trying to gain control of your people. He is a man who can wield fire, water, earth and air. We have a plan to stop him, but we need a Populous from each element to help us," Seth explains.

The woman laughs again. "And why exactly is he doing this?"

"We do not yet know."

"Well then you have nothing. Do you really expect me to just give you one of my Earth Populous to help you take down some unknown evil? Come to me when you have more proof of these events," she says, dismissing us with a wave of her hand.

We are led back to our boat by the man who led us here. Seth puts the boat into the water and motions for me to get in. I climb into the boat and sit down on the little wooden bench at the front. Seth pushes the boat out farther and quickly jumps in, careful not to touch the water. Behind Seth, the man walks away, his job done and the threat slowly rowing away.

"So what now?" I ask.

"Now we have to find proof, and fast, before the man gets more control over their Queen," Seth says.

"How?" I ask.

"By going back to the Fire Populous' island and figuring out more."

"We have to go back there *again*?" I say. I'm not looking forward to that at all.

"Yes. I'm guessing that that's where he'll be, since we just escaped and all. He'll probably be trying to gain more control to keep people from freaking out."

"But what if we get caught?"

"We don't have any other options, Rose."

"But what if he's not even there?" I say, still protesting.

"Then we look for him on one of the other islands," he says, clearly getting annoyed with my questions and worries.

I sigh and then lean back, looking back at the island as it slowly gets smaller. "Hey, their Queen never told us her name," I point out.

"Her name is Iridessa."

"That's an exotic name," I say.

After a while of driving, we arrive at the island. "Hurry, get off the boat and go and hide in the trees. I'll meet you there," Seth tells me.

I do as he says and hide in the trees, waiting for him to join me. I watch him quickly pull the boat out of the water and hide it in the bushes. When he joins me, I ask, "So what now?"

"It's getting dark, so I think we should find a place to sleep—somewhere they won't find us," he says, leading me deeper into the forest.

We walk for a few minutes until we reach a wall of vines and plants. I am about to ask Seth why we've stopped here at a dead end when he pulls some of the vines aside to reveal a cave hidden behind them. "We should be safe here for tonight," he says, entering the little cave.

I hadn't even noticed that Seth had brought our bags with him until he turns on a flashlight, illuminating the cave. The cave is pretty small, and it's empty except for some really gross, dirty blankets I'm assuming Seth left here. "Is this your little hideout?" I ask Seth in a joking tone of voice.

He laughs as he takes out a sleeping bag from his bag. "When I was younger, yeah. I have a feeling it's going to get pretty cold tonight without a fire." Seth lies down in his sleeping bag on the hard floor of the cave, resting his head on his arm.

Oh joy, I think to myself, *I get to sleep on a nice, comfortable cave floor.* I reach into my backpack and try to find a sleeping bag. When I can't find one, I say, "Seth, is there another sleeping bag in your bag? There isn't one in mine."

Seth sits up and checks his bag, "Nope, there's not another one in here."

"So what should I do?" I ask him.

Seth smirks and then says, "You can use those blankets over there." He shines the flashlight over where the gross blankets lay.

"Ew, no way!" I exclaim.

Seth laughs, hesitates and says, "I guess we'll have to share mine."

"Maybe if you unzipped it to make it like a blanket, we would have more room between us," I suggest.

Seth unzips the zipper, but because the zipper is too short the sleeping bag can't be made into a blanket. I think back to when Maria told me about Seth and I dining alone, and the knowing look she gave me. *Maria!* I think to myself. *She planned this!*

Seth zips the sleeping bag up halfway and then moves over, making room for me. I awkwardly and shyly slide into the sleeping bag beside him. The blue little sleeping bag is only a double one, so we have to lie pretty close together even though Seth is as far as he can go on his side of the sleeping bag. After I close the sleeping bag all the way, I go as far as I can go on the other side.

"Goodnight," Seth says quietly, and he turns off the flashlight, leaving the cave pitch black.

I clear my throat. "Good night." Then I go to sleep.

CHAPTER 12

The next day I open my eyes and see Seth's face very close to mine. Both of our heads are resting on his arm. Luckily he is still asleep. I slowly start to move away from him, careful not to wake him up.

After I am up, I take a peek outside. I move the curtain of vines out of my way and see that the sun is up. I squint my eyes while they get used to the brightness. Once my eyes have adjusted, I take a look at my watch: 11:30. I go back into the cave to wake up Seth.

I kneel down in front of him and gently shake him while saying, "Seth, wake up, we should get going now."

Seth slowly opens his eyes, sits up and stretches. "What time is it?" he asks.

"It's 11:30," I reply.

"We'd better hurry."

I follow Seth as he carefully leads us back to the Fire Populous' little village. "Stay close and stay quiet," he whispers to me.

"Shouldn't we be doing this at night?" I ask.

"Yeah, then we'd be able to watch them sleep," Seth says sarcastically.

I sigh and continue to follow him.

He leads me to behind the prison where he was once held prisoner. Then he says, "Stay here."

"While you do what?"

"While I find out what this guy is after."

"No way," I say. "We're in this together. I'm coming with you."

"Rose, you need to trust me on this. What I'm about to do is not something you need to see."

"I don't care," I say. "Whatever it is, I'm sure I can handle it." I stand my ground and refuse to be left behind.

"Fine," Seth says, "but don't say I didn't warn you."

Seth starts walking towards the main building; I haven't really had the chance to see it during my short stay here. It is a large building, made mainly out of wood. It's shaped kind of like a giant house. The only thing that gives away the fact that important people live in there are the guards who stand outside the doors.

I follow Seth as he sneaks around to the back. There are guards there as well. Seth pauses for a while, probably thinking of the best way to get in undetected. After a moment he's on the move again.

Seth stops just at the edge of the woods and motions for me to stand in front of him. I slowly move to where he points. Then all of a sudden Seth pushes me out of the bushes and into plain sight of the guards.

The guards turn towards me and start to close in. I turn and start running back towards where Seth was for protection, but he is no longer there. I panic and pick up my pace. With the guards on my heels, I run as fast as I can through the forest, silently cursing Seth for betraying me like this. I trusted him!

There are so many tree roots and tree trunks in my way, and I can barely keep my footing. All of a sudden, I trip over a tree root and fall flat on my face. Seconds later, the guards are picking me up. They turn and start to bring me back the way we came. *I am so dead*—I think to myself.

Then all of a sudden I hear two thuds, and the guards fall to the ground. I turn around and see Seth standing behind me with a large tree branch in his hand. I glare at him. Unfazed, he smirks at me and starts walking back the way we came. I decide to let it go for now, but he will definitely be hearing about this later.

We reach the main building and enter the now unguarded door. Seth quickly finds a giant plant to hide behind. When he sees there is no one there, he walks up a set of winding stairs. We walk up carefully and quietly.

At the top, there is a hallway leading to a large door. We approach it, and Seth slowly opens it and peeks in. Then he sighs and then walks in. I follow and see why he is sighing: there is no one there.

"Looks like we won't be eavesdropping like I'd hoped," he says.

"Wait, you said I wouldn't be able to handle what you were planning to do."

"Yeah, but then you insisted on coming, so I decided to change tactics and hope we were lucky enough to be able to catch them talking about their plan. But now I guess we'll have to go with my original plan." Seth turns to leave.

"Which is?" I ask

"You'll see," he says as he heads back downstairs.

We return to the cave and sit. "What now?" I ask.

"Now we eat and wait until dark. Then we need to go back to the main building and grab the King's advisor. He'll know what's going on," Seth says, pulling out a granola bar from his bag and eating it. I do the same.

After I'm done eating, I lean back on the cave wall. We don't need our flashlights because of the light that filters in through the cracks in the vines. I look at Seth as he leans on his elbows and looks at me. "What?" I ask.

"You know I plan on torturing the King's advisor for information, right?" he asks.

"Well, I do now, but I'm still not going to stay behind," I say stubbornly.

"Fine, whatever."

"So what was the big idea, using me as bait?" I ask, suddenly remembering what he did.

He laughs. "The idea was to lure the guards into the forest, so I could kill them."

"Well, you could have let me in on the plan."

Seth laughs again. "If I had done that, it wouldn't have been so funny."

I glare at him, "That was really mean. I thought you had actually left me, and they were going to kill me." Tears start to run down my cheeks.

Seth looks at me, sees me crying and immediately stops laughing. He slides over to me and leans on the cave wall next to me. Then he shyly puts his arm around me and pulls me close. I bury my face in the crook of his neck and cry. After everything that has happened, this is the first time I've let myself cry about it. Of course, it's in front of Seth, of all people.

After a little while, I pull away just enough to look at him. "Why are you being so nice to me?" I ask.

"Because I can't stand seeing a girl cry," Seth says in a teasing tone and wipes a tear from my face.

I lean my head back against his neck and put my arms around him, pulling myself closer, not wanting this moment to end just yet because I'm not sure when he'll hold me like this again. *Which is fine with me,* I think to myself, even though I know for a fact that it is not true.

We stay like that, in each other's arms, until the sun sets and it's time to go and get the Fire Populous King's advisor.

"Wait here; I'll be right back," Seth whispers into my ear.

"What are you going to do?" I ask suspiciously as he gets up and grabs our bags.

"Calm down. I'm just going to bring our bags to the boat. After this, we're going to need a quick getaway." When I don't respond, he leaves.

Seth returns and we head out. Once we get back to the main building, we head to the back and do the same thing we did before: we lure the guards into the forest, using me as bait, and then Seth kills them.

Once we're back in the main building, we hide behind the same plant as before. Seth checks to make sure the coast is clear, and then we start carefully searching for the King's advisor's bedroom. *I never did learn his name,* I think to myself.

Seth and I split up to cover more ground, unsure of the amount of time we have. "Over here," Seth says eventually.

I close the door to the room that I had just been looking in and go to where Seth is waiting for me. It takes a little bit for me to get to him, because it is quite dark in the building, with only the light from the moon coming in through the windows. *Everyone must be asleep,* I think to myself.

Seth creeps into the room, and I follow. We sneak to the side of the King's advisor's bed, and Seth knocks him out before he can even really wake up. Then Seth throws him over his shoulder and we leave. We run through the trees, back towards the shore where our boat is. Seth grabs chains from the boat and ties the man up. Then we wait.

When the man finally comes to, Seth cuts to the chase. "What do you know about the man who can wield fire, water, earth and air?"

"I know that he will kill you when he finds out you're here."

"Trust me; we'll be gone before that happens," Seth says. "Now tell me, what is he planning?"

"You mean Luther? I will tell you nothing!" the advisor exclaims.

"I think you will," Seth says, punching the man in the face.

I cringe and look away.

"Is that all you've got?" the man says as he spits up blood.

I stare at the blood in astonishment. It doesn't look like blood at all. It looks like . . . lava! It's yellow and gives off light like a fire. *That's what's inside of him, of Seth, of me?* I think to myself as I look at the seemingly normal looking veins on my arms. *At least they look normal from the outside! I wonder what they look like on the inside. I wonder what they're made of!*

I'm brought back to high alert when I hear the man grunting again. I look back at Seth, who is still trying to beat information out of the man. The man continues to spit out blood or whatever it is, and he is now cursing at Seth. Seth continues to punch and kick him, but he won't tell us a thing.

"Seth, he's not going to tell us anything," I say.

"Oh yes he will," Seth says, rolling the man towards the water.

"Stop! You won't get away with this!" the advisor yells, struggling to get out of the metal, fireproof chains that bind him.

Seth continues to roll him towards the water. I cringe as he gets closer and closer, remembering how agonizing it is to feel the water on my skin.

Just as the man is about to touch the water, he finally gives in. "Fine! I'll tell you what you want! Just get me away from the water!"

Seth pulls the man away from the water. When the man says nothing, Seth raises one eyebrow and says, "Well? What are you waiting for? Tell us what you know."

The man clears his throat and then says, "I know that he is planning to control all of the leaders of each Populous."

"We already know that!" Seth yells.

"I also know that he's using some potion from the spell books we have here on the island to do it."

"Do you know why?" Seth prompts.

"He wants to start a war that will wipe us all out, and he plans to finish off whoever's left," the man says with a voice filled with hate towards us.

"Why does he want us all dead?" Seth asks.

"He wants to rule over the humans. He knows that the Populous' would never let him rule over them, and he can't cast a spell that strong on all of us. Even he's not powerful enough for that. He can only influence us enough to make us start a war against each other."

"Who's to say the humans will let him? They have developed some pretty strong weapons. Some can kill us."

The man laughs. "You're forgetting that with all of the other Populous' dead, not only will there be no one to stop him, but there will be no Populous to create the elements necessary for human survival except for him."

"Of course," Seth says to himself. "They need fire for warmth and light, water for hydration, air to breath and earth to live on. Without at least one Populous for each of the elements, there will be no one to provide it for them."

"And with all of the Populous' dead except for him, they'll have no choice but to serve him, or they'll die, too," the man says. "There, I've told you everything I know. Now let me go!"

"You don't seem to be under a spell to me," Seth observes.

"That's because I'm not!" the advisor yells.

"Then why are you helping this man wipe us all out?"

"Because he said he would let me live, and he would give me a position of great power over the humans. Now let me go!"

"What was his original power?" Seth asks.

"Fire!" the man exclaims. "That's all I know! Now let me go!"

"What does he look like?" Seth asks.

"There's a picture of him in my pocket!"

Seth takes out the picture, takes a look and hands it to me.

I examine the picture quickly before putting it in my pocket. The man is quite ugly. He is pale and bald, with a scar that goes from his chin to over his eye—which is not there—all the way up to his head. His face wears a grimace.

"Why do you have a picture of him in your pocket?" Seth asks.

"Because I've never seen him face to face. This way I don't accidentally kill him," he replies. "Now, let me go!" He kicks and thrashes against his binds, which is no use because he's too weak and scrawny to shake them off.

"So you can run back and get the guards before we have a chance to leave? I don't think so," Seth says, getting more chains from the boat and tying the man securely to a tree. "Come on, let's go." Seth grabs my arm and helps me into the boat. He pushes off and jumps in, always careful not to touch the water.

CHAPTER 13

*a*s Seth rows us back to the Earth Populous' island, I stare at him and wonder why I'm not afraid of him after seeing what he was capable of. As if he could read my thoughts, he says, "I told you it would be bad, did I not?" He immediately goes on the defensive. Apparently, he didn't guess *exactly* what I was thinking.

"It didn't scare me, Seth," I say. "You didn't scare me. And you still don't." He doesn't reply. "What colour is the other Populous' blood?" I ask.

"What?" Seth asks, looking at me as if he thinks I'm going crazy.

"That guy's blood was yellow," I say.

"Oh, that. Well, the Earth Populous' blood is bright green, the Air Populous' blood is white, and the Water Populous' blood is dark blue, even after it mixes with the air."

"That's cool and weird at the same time," I say, looking at my veins again. "How come our veins don't look different from the outside?"

"How am I supposed to know?" Seth says. "Why can we wield fire? How do we sustain the life of humans just by being? How do we turn into fire without burning or dying? All very good questions for which no one has answers."

"Whoa, we can turn *into* fire?" I ask, fascinated with that possibility.

"Oh, yeah, I keep forgetting that you were raised as a human."

"It wasn't so bad," I say, trying to defend myself even though I know for a fact that I never really enjoyed simply being a human.

Seth rolls his eyes. "Anyways, yes, we can turn into fire. It takes a lot of concentration, but once you get it, it's an amazing experience, flying through the sky as fire."

"You can *fly* when you're fire?"

"That's what I just said, isn't it?"

I cross my arms in front of my chest. "Yes." I look away from him and out at the ocean.

Once we get to the Earth Populous' island, we get out and head back to what I assume is their throne room. The guards outside lead us to the throne where their Queen sits. "You are back already?" she asks.

I look at Seth and wait for him to speak. "Yes, we are back with the information you asked for," Seth says.

"Go on, tell me what you have discovered," Queen Iridessa says.

Seth tells her what the advisor told him. When he is finished, she sits there silently. When I look into her eyes, I see what appears to be a battle going on inside of her. It's as if she wants to do one thing, but something won't let her. *The potion,* I think to myself.

Queen Iridessa finally says, "I'm afraid there is nothing we can do. I advise you to leave now".

Seth quickly grabs my arm, and we head out. He leads me to one of the trees with a tree house on it and tells me to climb up the ladder that is there.

After I'm up, he does the same. "What are we doing?" I ask as he knocks on the door.

"Recruiting."

The door opens, and a beautiful woman about my age opens the door. She looks like a real-life Pocahontas, only she wears an outfit that consists of a white bikini-type top with a green gem in the middle and a green skirt. The dull green of her skirt brings out the green in her hazel eyes. When I look down at her arms, I see intricate green tattoos twisting up her arms. She looks like a warrior princess.

"Do I know you?" she asks with a confused look on her face.

"We need your help," Seth says.

"My help with what?" she asks, now measuring us both and deciding whether she can take us.

"Do you know where Keith is?" Seth asks.

"Yes," she says.

"Where is he?"

"He's dropping off some papers at the main building. Why?" She is still watching our every move.

"Will he be back soon?" Seth asks, ignoring her question.

"Yes. Why?" she asks, this time more firmly.

"Because, we need to speak with him. It's important."

"What the hell is going on? Who are you?" she asks, getting more and more upset.

"I'm Seth, and this is Rose," Seth answers.

"Seth? Keith has told me about you," She says, relaxing a little.

"Yeah, and he's told me about you. It's nice to know he finally got you to admit that you are his soul mate," Seth says, smiling.

"Yes," she replies, her expression changing to one of pure love for a second, before it is gone.

"Your soul mate?" I ask.

"Yes, my soul mate," she says as if it's the most trivial thing in the world.

I look at Seth with a questioning gaze. He looks back at me and whispers, "I'll tell you later." He turns his attention back to the woman. "We need you to help us save all of the Populous." Then he explains everything that has happened during the last few days.

"And you want Keith to help kill this man?" the woman asks.

"Yes."

"You'll have to take me with you. There is no way he is going on this adventure without me."

"When will he be home?" Seth asks.

"He should be home soon; it's almost dinner time."

"Do you mind if we wait here?"

"Sure," she replies and motions for us to follow her into her house.

We head through a short hallway and around a corner. She stops in front of a small room with wood floors and a wooden table, with a red sofa and a loveseat around it. There is a cute little fire place in front of them. She motions for us to sit, and we do as she says. "I'm Elaina, by the way," she says. "Make yourself at home; if you'll excuse me for a minute, I just need to put dinner in the oven."

I turn to look at Seth, who is sitting on the other side of the couch from me. "So, what's a soul mate?" I ask Seth after she is gone.

"It's when two Populous' fall in love at first sight," Seth says as Elaina walks back in.

"That's not true," Elaina says. "A soul mate is the Populous you were made for: You complete each other, balance each other out. There is one for everyone, and it is not always love at first sight. It's different for everyone. For some it is in fact love at first sight, for some it takes more time and for others it is something that is thrust upon them, something they can't help even if they hate each other, even if they are enemies."

"What was it like for you and your soul mate?" I ask her, thinking how wonderful and romantic it must be to have one.

"For us, it took some convincing—mostly him convincing me," she says. "I don't know if you've noticed, but I'm a very independent woman, so naturally I did not like the idea of having a soul mate, but a soul mate is someone you cannot resist, no matter how much you may want to."

"But you're happy now, right?" I ask her.

"Yes, I'm very happy now," she says, smiling.

"How do you know if someone's your soul mate? What does it feel like?" I ask, genuinely curious about the subject.

"Like I said before, it's different for everyone, but for me it was like there was this connection that kept getting stronger and stronger. I tried to deny it, to make it go away and stay away from him, but it just got harder to do so, especially because he was pursuing me. Then finally, one day I couldn't deny it anymore. The day I finally gave in to it, to him, was the best day of my life, the first day of forever with him."

I sigh, thinking how wonderful it must be for her and how happy she must be. "I hope I find my soul mate," I say, and then I blush, remembering that Seth is here.

Elaina smiles. "I think you already have."

"Huh?" I ask.

"I would love to tell you to speed things up, but a soul mate is someone you must recognize by yourself," she says.

Just then, I hear the front door open. A few seconds later, a tall, very muscular, tan man with black hair and brown eyes comes in. Elaina gets up from the loveseat she was sitting on and hugs her soul mate. He quickly picks her up and twirls her around, giving her a kiss, unfazed by the people sitting on his couch and watching the show of affection.

Once he puts her down, Elaina motions to us. "Keith, Seth and Rose have some information they would like to share with us, and they have come to seek our help."

"Seth?" Keith says. "Is that you?"

"Yeah," Seth replies.

"It's good to see you. I haven't seen you in years."

"I know; I've been a little busy," Seth lies.

"Well, you'll have to explain to me what you've been busy with later," Keith says, looking from Seth to me. I blush.

"I see you've been busy, too. You finally won Elaina's heart," Seth tells him.

"Yep, it took a lot of hard work, but in the end it was worth it." Keith looks at Elaina lovingly.

After a few moments go by, Seth clears his throat.

Keith looks at us, his attention on us again as he sits down on the loveseat. Elaina sits down beside him, and he puts his arm around her, pulling her close to him.

Seth explains what we have come here for and why. His explanation also answers Keith's earlier question of where he has been all these years. Once Seth is done, Keith says, "I believe you, and I have seen evidence of some of these events—like the way our Queen has been acting of late. However, I refuse to let Elaina put herself in danger like that. I will go alone, and she will stay here."

Elaina pulls away from Keith so she can face him. "I don't think so. I said I would only let you go if I could go, too."

"Sorry, Elaina, but you're not going, and that's final."

"Since when do you order me around?" Elaina says, raising her voice a little and putting her hands on her hips—both signs that she is not about to give in.

Just as Keith is about to say something back, I step in. "You could both come. Elaina will be fine. I have been accompanying Seth, and I can guarantee you that Elaina is a much better warrior than I am."

They both look at me as if they had forgotten we were here.

"Then it's settled, we both go," Elaina says.

"We will leave in the morning," Keith agrees.

"Until then, you two are welcome to stay here," Elaina finishes.

"Thank you," Seth and I say.

"Would you like to help me finish dinner?" Elaina asks me.

"Sure," I say, even though I don't really cook.

I follow Elaina into the kitchen. She gets to work cooking, and I awkwardly stand there, not sure what to do. "Here," Elaina says, handing me a cutting board, a knife and some vegetables. "You can cut the vegetables for the salad."

I take them, set them on the table and start cutting.

"So tell me about yourself," Elaina says as she sits down with some corn and shucks it.

"Um, I was raised thinking I was a human, not knowing any of this existed until I accidentally let Seth out of this room in my house. My parents locked him in there. He tried to kill me using fire, and my parents brought me to an island where there's a whole village of people who could wield fire. Then it all went downhill from there," I say. "Sometimes I wonder why all of this is happening to me."

"Everything happens for a reason," Elaina says, not at all looking like my story is that bizarre to her.

"Do you by any chance know what that reason is?" I ask, only half joking.

Elaina smiles. "I think I may have an idea."

"Will you tell me, or do I have to figure it out?" I ask.

"You're going to have to figure it out by yourself."

We continue to prepare dinner while we talk. We talk about regular stuff like men, family, fashion and makeup. For a moment it almost feels like my life is normal again—as though the recent life-changing events never took place.

Once we are finished cooking, we call Seth and Keith for dinner, and then we eat in the living room while we watch TV. After we eat, we clean up our dishes and stuff.

"You and Seth will have to share the bed in our guest room. I wasn't exactly expecting visitors," Elaina says apologetically.

"That's all right," I say.

"Follow me, then," she says, leading us to the guest room.

When we get there, I immediately see the size of the bed; it looks like it's a double bed. Great. The rest of the room is also quite small but in a neat, cozy way. The walls and floor are wood, and the bedspread is beige. The only decor are brown, wooden side tables on each side of the bed, with a lamp on each of them. There is a little closet on the wall opposite of the bed.

"I hope this will be all right," Elaina says.

"Yeah, it's good," I say, trying to be polite.

I crawl onto the bed and slip under the covers. Seth looks at me and then turns around, closes the bedroom door, and just stands there awkwardly. I'm so tired and know that tomorrow will be another busy day, so I just shrug, lie down on my side, and close my eyes.

A few seconds later, I feel the bed shift as Seth gets in. I open my eyes to find that the light is off. After my eyes adjust, I can see Seth lying there next to me on his back.

"You and Keith are friends?" I ask.

"Yeah. My parents liked to visit the other Populous' sometimes—except for the Water Populous, of course."

Leaving the conversation at that, I close my eyes again and let sleep take hold.

Chapter 14

The next day, I wake up and see that the spot where Seth was sleeping is empty. I walk to the living room and see that no one is there. I head to the kitchen and find Elaina making pancakes. When she sees me, she says, "Seth and Keith are getting the boats ready."

"Boats?" I ask, wondering if she knows that we only came with one.

"Yes. They went and grabbed two motor boats and are now getting them ready to go." She replies.

When Seth and Keith return, we eat breakfast and then head out. We walk to the shore and climb into the boats, Seth and I in one and Elaina and Keith in the other.

Seth and Keith start the boats, and we are quickly whisked out to sea, heading in what I assume is the direction of the Water Populous' island. "This must be much easier than rowing," I say.

"Yeah, much. I barely have to do anything," Seth replies.

I laugh and then sit back and enjoy the ride.

Later, when we are near enough to the island for me to be able to see all of its details and not just a giant blob of green; I see that their houses are set up a lot differently than the other Populous' islands. Their houses are all at the edge of the island, close to the water. *They* are *the Water*

Populous, after all, I think to myself. The only ways in on this side of the island are the docks, which are off to the side a bit. I assume that when we escaped from the Fire Populous' island, we entered their island on the other side. Behind all of the houses is a jungle of trees and plants. The houses themselves are like the rest of the Populous' houses, made with natural materials.

As we approach the docks, Seth says to me, "Don't let them know you're a Fire Populous—they may not like that so much." Then he pulls the sleeves of his black long-sleeved shirt down to cover his tattoo.

"All right."

We dock our boats and get out on the docks. We are immediately greeted by a short, pale man with short dark hair. He wears blue pants and no shirt, making it easy to see lots of his blue, intricate tattoos. He has a bit of a gut, but he obviously does not care because he makes no attempt to conceal it. "Who are you?" he asks us.

I look at Elaina and Keith, who are wearing the same clothes as yesterday. Elaina is now wearing short black boots, and Keith is wearing green pants, a black vest, and black boots. Before we left Elaina and Keith's place, Seth and I borrowed some of their clothes so we would look like we are Earth Populous. I borrowed a green top from Elaina and some tight black pants and green shoes. Seth borrowed Keith's only long-sleeved black shirt and some green pants and boots.

"We are Earth Populous, here to speak to you about some very serious matters," Seth says.

"In that case, follow me," the man says, turning and not even looking back to see if we are following.

We follow. While he leads us to wherever he is taking us, we all look around. I see trees, flowers and Water Populous who are looking at us with curious gazes. Some of them are in the water and wearing blue swimsuits. The ones who aren't staring at us are manipulating water and making it dance around. I look away uneasily.

The man stops at a small, empty, circular clearing surrounded by trees. The only things in the clearing are a long bench and an unlit torch beside it. The man sits down. The rest of us just stand awkwardly in front of him, not sure what to do. "You may say what you wanted to tell me," he says.

Seth tells him what we know, though it's a little bit more edited, probably because of how arrogant this man seems. His mind is probably easily controlled. Seth tells him about the man, what we think his plans are and how we can destroy him. Then he finally asks for a single Water Populous to help us.

I look at the man while he thinks about what Seth just said. I see a little battle in his eyes, but it is nothing compared to the battle that I saw going on in Queen Iridessa's eyes. Before we know it, he stands up and says, "I feel there is no real threat, and so I will not provide you with one of my Water Populous to aid you." Then he leaves.

"What now?" I ask.

"I don't know," Seth says. "I doubt the Water Populous will be as easy to convince as Keith and Elaina were. I don't have any ties with them, for obvious reasons."

"Keith, do you or Elaina know any Water Populous who can help us?" I ask.

"No," Keith says regrettably.

"I'm afraid not," Elaina confirms, shaking her head.

All of a sudden we hear, "I know someone who can help you." Then seconds later, I see a man emerging from the trees.

As he gets closer, I see him more clearly. He is quite different than Keith and Seth, with blonde hair and blue eyes that hold a mischievous look. He is just as tall as Seth and is almost as muscled as Keith. His hair is long with wavy curls through which any girl would love to run their fingers. His skin is lightly tanned; I can tell because he only wears a blue swimsuit that clearly shows off his tight abs, strong arms and defined chest. His face is just as good looking as the rest of him and is perfectly symmetrical. His features are soft but just defined enough to keep him from looking like a cute little boy. He also has a little bit of stubble to prove he is no child. His blue tattoos make the muscles on his arms look even more defined.

"Huh?" I ask brilliantly, still staring.

He smirks, reminding me of the way Seth always smiles, except this guy smirks in a different way than Seth: his has more of an amused, mischievous smirk.

I smile at him shyly.

"Allow me to introduce myself," he says, coming closer and reaching out to grab my hand. "I am Lucas." He leans down and kisses the back of my hand. He does the same thing to Elaina before continuing. "And I am here to help you with your little . . . predicament." He bows dramatically before us.

I smile at his boyish charm. I look over and see Elaina doing the same.

Keith and Seth both say, "We don't need your help," at the same time. They're obviously not nearly as charmed by Lucas as Elaina and I.

"That's not what I heard," Lucas says, smirking.

"Yeah, that's not what I heard, either," I say, looking first at Elaina, and then at Seth and Keith.

"Face it, I'm probably the only Water Populous here crazy enough to even consider helping you," Lucas says. "Unless, of course, you want to stay here for who knows how long, trying to gain someone's trust. By then it could already be too late."

"He's right," I say. "And besides, I don't know what your guys' problem is. He looks fit for the job."

"Fine, whatever," Seth says, turning and heading back to the docks with Keith, neither of them waiting for the rest of us.

Lucas shrugs and then holds out his arms for Elaina and me to put our arms through. We look at each other, shrug, put our arms through his and then follow.

Back at the docks, we get in the boats, Elaina and Keith in one and Seth, Lucas and I in the other. We head back to the Air Populous island to get Maria.

"So, what is it exactly that makes you crazy enough to come with us?" I ask Lucas.

"Well, let's just say I'm known for being a reckless risk-taker," Lucas says, avoiding eye contact.

"And what did you do to earn that reputation?"

"I'd rather not get into it," Lucas replies.

"Is it something bad?" Seth asks harshly. "Something we should know about?"

"No," is all Lucas says.

"No to which question?" Seth asks, not letting up. Lucas doesn't answer. Seth looks angry. "This conversation isn't over." He is probably planning to bring it up when he has Keith to help pry the information out of Lucas.

"Just let it go, Seth," I say. "As long as it won't affect what we're trying to do, it's none of our business."

Seth doesn't answer, but by the very serious, cold look he has on his face, he doesn't care if it isn't his business—he plans to *make* it his business.

The rest of the ride to the island is spent in silence, all of us looking at different parts of the ocean and avoiding eye contact with one another.

When we finally get there, I go to jump out of the boat and almost fall into the water, but luckily for me Lucas grabs my hand and pulls me back into the boat, and into his strong arms.

"Thanks," I say, my breathing speeding up a little.

"No problem," he says. "You'd better be more careful next time, though. I hear Fire Populous don't really like water all that much." He smirks.

Realizing that he is still holding me in his arms, I pull away, checking to see if Seth saw. I see Seth over by Keith and when he looks over at me

I can tell he did by the way his features have turned even colder than they were before.

I look back at Lucas, realizing that I had never told him that I was a Fire Populous; there was no way he should have known. In fact, if I remember correctly, I was specifically told not to tell any of the Water Populous that I was one. "How did you know that I am a Fire Populous?" I ask.

"Just a lucky guess. From what you told me, you needed a Populous from each element, so I figured one of you had to be one," Lucas says, shrugging.

"And that doesn't bother you?" I ask.

"Nope."

When he doesn't continue, I ask, "Why not?"

Before he can hide it, I see a distant, regretful and troubled look cross his face. It only lasts for a brief moment before it is replaced by his signature smirk. "Because I hear the women are really hot," he says.

I grimace. "Seriously? That's the best pickup line you could come up with for a Fire Populous? Sorry, but you'll have to try harder," I say smiling at him to show that I'm joking.

Lucas gets off the boat and gently helps me off, making sure I don't touch the water.

"Hey!" I hear off to my left. I look over and see Maria running over to us with a worried look on her face.

"What is it?" Seth asks her once she reaches us.

"It's the Air Populous! They're searching the whole island for you guys!" she says, unfolding a piece of paper she had in her hands and showing it to us. We all take a look and go silent. The picture is a wanted sign with a picture of me and Seth on it.

"What do they want with us?" I ask.

"I'll explain later, but first we have to get out of here," Maria says, already jumping into one of the boats.

"Lucas, you'll have to ride with Keith and Elaina," Seth says.

"Okay," Lucas says, jumping into the other boat where Keith and Elaina wait.

As soon as Lucas is in, Keith starts the boat and heads out, not stopping to wait for us until he is at a distance from the island.

"Come on, there isn't much time! The whole island is looking for you!" Maria yells urgently to us.

Seth helps me in the boat, pushes off and jumps in, not quite able to avoid the waves that are rolling in. Seth cringes as some water splashes onto his leg. He doesn't stop or even slow down, though. He quickly starts the engine, and we all but fly away from the island.

Unfortunately for us, we aren't yet far enough away for the Air Populous' powers. There are a bunch of them at the edge of the island, throwing wind at us. I didn't think it would do much—it is air, after all—but the force of it is so great that the waves they are creating are huge and heading straight for us at great speed. There is no way for us to get out of their way.

As the waves get closer and closer, I start to panic. When those waves hit us, Seth and I will go flying into the painful, waiting waters below.

I close my eyes and wait for the one closest to us to hit, for the searing pain that will follow closely behind. But when a couple of minutes go by, I open my eyes to see what the holdup is. When I do, I see the giant wave is now being pushed in the other direction, and it is getting smaller and smaller, merging with the rest of the water beneath us.

I turn and see Lucas standing in the other boat, sweat trickling down his forehead as he tries to keep the onslaught of waves under control and away from us.

"Drive!" I yell, only now realizing that both of the boats have stopped. Seth immediately does as I say and speeds away.

I look behind me and see Elaina grabbing hold of Lucas to keep him from falling into the water as Keith follows quickly behind us.

CHAPTER 15

"Maria, what happened back there? Why are they after us?" Seth asks once we are floating in the middle of the ocean. Keith, Elaina and Lucas are right beside us, holding on to our boat so they don't float away.

"I don't know all of the details, but I heard something about one of the leaders of the Fire Populous being tortured for information by you guys," Maria says, pausing to look at us questioningly. "The reward they have put on your capture is a very generous amount."

"If everyone is after you, then where are we supposed to go to train?" Keith asks.

"Train?" I ask. "Why do we need to train?"

"Because the books say there is a certain way we have to kill him. We may be running out of time, but we'll only have one shot at this, and we can't blow it," Seth replies. "And Keith, I have no idea where we can go, but I know we can't go back to any of the islands—they're probably all on high alert."

"We could go to where the humans live," I say, not sure what I should call it.

"Yes, we'll go there," Seth says.

We go to the dock where I originally left for the Fire Populous island. At the time I was running from Seth. It's ironic how now I'm running away from my parents, and with Seth.

We all get out of our boats and start walking. "Where are we going?" I ask.

"I don't know. It's too dangerous to go back to your house, and we don't have any other place to stay, so we'll probably have to hide in the woods." Seth says.

"Our backpacks!" I say, remembering the bags Maria had packed us.

"Here," Maria says, handing them to us. "You forgot them in the boat."

"Thanks," I say, taking mine.

Seth takes his and then says, "It won't be enough for everyone."

"We could run to my house and grab some stuff." I suggest.

"All right, but we'll have to make sure there are no Fire Populous guarding your house," Seth says.

Once we get to my house, we check for guards. When we find no one, we walk up to the door. I open the door and let out a sigh of relief. The door was left unlocked. I kind of figured it would be because my parents and I left in a major hurry.

We head inside and start grabbing a bunch of blankets, pillows and any other things we may need. I head upstairs, following the holes Seth left in the walls when he was trying to kill me. I can't believe how wrong I had it when I first found him, and how wrong he had been when he had first seen me.

I enter the room that held the door he was locked behind for all those years, and I see that Seth is already in here, standing in front of the now open door, simply staring at the room.

I turn around and start to leave so he can have privacy, but I feel his hand holding my arm, stopping me from leaving. "Thank you," he says.

"What?"

"I never did thank you for freeing me, so thank you."

"You're welcome," I say, permitting myself to look into his eyes. The eyes I have avoided for some time. The eyes I remember as black as a dark, moonless, starless night. However, when I look into them now, I see that they are not black but a beautiful, dark, chocolate brown.

I start to slowly lean in, longing to feel his lips on mine. He may be obnoxious and arrogant on the surface, but that guise is only to hide the pain and loss and fear he has felt during his years. I have seen what lies underneath; no matter how briefly those moments may have lasted, I know what I saw. I saw a loving, strong man who is constantly struggling with the events of his past, the events in which my parents had a hand. Those brief moments where he opened up were some of the best moments of my life.

I've always wanted an adventure, and I have it now. He is my adventure.

Seth starts leaning in as well. I can see the longing in his eyes. I can also see the resistance, and I know why it's there. It's there because he doesn't want to love, because to him, if he loves, then there is a chance to lose and to hurt if it is ever taken away. He is scared to love.

Just as our lips are about to finally touch, I hear Keith calling for us. "Come on, hurry up! We've got to go!"

Seth quickly pulls away and leaves the room. I stand there for a moment, staring at the door Seth just walked out of, and then I follow, grabbing supplies on the way to the front door.

We walk to the woods by my house. We live in a tropical place, so there is a lot of jungle in which to hide. We walk for what feels like an hour. When we finally stop, I drop all of the supplies that I grabbed and plop down to rest.

Maria and Elaina lay down beside me as Keith, Lucas and Seth start setting up a shelter for us. Once the shelter—which consists of a big, blue tarp strapped to some trees and blankets spread out on the ground—is set up, we start preparing for the battle ahead.

"The spell books say that there is a certain way to do this," Seth says, pacing in front of Keith, Elaina, Maria, Lucas and I, who are standing in a line in front of him. "We must all use our powers against him." Seth pauses and looks at Elaina and Keith. "Only one of you can do this."

"I will," they say at the same time.

Before they can start arguing about it, I interject. "How about we all train, and then you two can discuss who will fight the guy later."

"Anyways," Seth says, "we need one Water Populous, one Air Populous, one Earth Populous and one extremely powerful Fire Populous, because his original power is fire."

"Okay, we have all of that, so let's go!" I say, no longer able to hide my impatience.

"I told you, we can't! We only have one shot at this so we have to get it right," Seth replies. "First off, we'll start by assuming he's still at the Fire Populous' island. If so, we'll have to sneak in the way Rose and I did the first time: get on from the back, travel through the forest and then take out the guards guarding the King's house. If he's at the Air Populous' island, we'll have to go in by Maria's house and sneak to their main building that way. For the Water Populous' island, we'll have to get in from the back, and then get to the other side by cutting through the middle. And finally, for the Earth Populous' island, we'll have to get in from the back and follow Keith and Elaina carefully, so we don't step on any of the plants around the perimeter to let them know we are there."

"Alright, now that that's settled, let's get on with it." I say.

Seth throws me a look, telling me to keep quiet. "To kill him, we have to use our powers in a certain order. First will be Air, then Water, then Earth and then finally Fire. Then we'll have to finish him off using this." He pulls out the Cinquedea des Morts for everyone to see.

"Alright, sounds easy enough," Lucas says.

"For the rest of the day, we can train and practice fighting with each other. Pair up and train," Seth says.

Elaina and Keith obviously pair up, and Lucas and Maria pair up, leaving Seth and I to practice with each other.

Seth leads me a few paces away from the others so we don't get in their way. "You remember what to do, right?" Seth asks me.

"Yeah," I say, remembering what he told me that day on the beach when he had escaped from the Fire Populous' prison.

I focus on the anger and betrayal I feel towards my parents. I know it's working and that a fireball is going to shoot out of my hand at any moment, because I can feel the heat running through my arm and to my hand.

After a few seconds, the fireball materializes and flies towards Seth. Unfortunately, the power in the fireball is quite weak, because before it can reach Seth, who is standing only 20 yards away, it slowly burns out until there is nothing left.

"It's okay, try again," Seth says, trying to encourage me.

This time I take a deep breath, close my eyes and really think about what my parents have done to me, and to Seth. I think about how every night I hope and pray that the only reason they have done all of the horrible things they have is because of the spell the man we are trying to defeat has cast upon them. I think about how my whole life was a giant lie because of them, how I grew up not knowing that I am capable of wielding fire, or about the island that holds others like me. But most of all, I hate what they have done to Seth, how they killed his parents and then locked him in a room for five years, how they have scarred him for life. I am so ashamed to even call them my parents.

This time, the heat I feel in my veins becomes hotter and hotter until my arm starts to tingle. This time the heat isn't originating from only my arm but from my whole body. The power being put into this fireball becomes greater and greater; all of the tingling heat from my body is flowing to my hand. Finally I open my eyes, take aim and shoot the fireball from my hand.

This fireball is much bigger than the last and makes it all the way to Seth, where he jumps out of the way at the last second. The fireball hits the tree Seth was standing in front of only moments ago. After it hits, the fireball leaves a medium-size hole in the tree, and the trunk is now ablaze with the fire that I created.

"Should I get Lucas to put it out?" I ask.

"No, come here," Seth says, moving towards the tree.

I do as he says. "Now what?"

"Watch," Seth says, moving his hand towards the fire I set on the tree. Seth touches the fire, and all of a sudden, the fire is flowing into Seth like he's absorbing it. Then he reignites the fire. "Concentrate on bringing the energy of the fire back into you, and focus on absorbing the heat and warmth."

I put my hand on the fire and do as he says. The next thing I know, the fire is gone. I absorbed it right back into me! I smile at Seth excitedly, and he smiles back.

I make a decision then and there that I am going to try to kiss him again. I lean in and start to close my eyes, anticipating the moment our lips will finally meet, but unlike all of the other times, he does not follow my lead. Instead he takes a step away from me and says, "We should keep practicing. You take way too long to shoot the fire. If you were actually fighting someone, you'd be dead before you could even begin the process of making the fireball."

I stare at him for a moment, confused. When he just stares back, obviously not about to give any kind of explanation, I walk farther away, and we take turns throwing fireballs and absorbing them. We do this in silence.

"Come here," Seth says after about an hour of practicing. I walk over towards him. "Now I'll show you how to move fire and wield it like a wave."

"Like a wave?" I repeat.

"What I mean is making it flow towards something or someone continuously," Seth says. "Like this." He makes a fire in the palm of his hand, but instead of turning it into a ball, he makes it rise and move like a snake, one long line of continuous fire. "To attack someone with it, you would obviously aim and use a lot more power. Can you see how this would hurt someone maybe more than the fireball?"

"Yeah. It would be a continuous attack with no time to escape—like being on fire," I answer.

"Exactly. Although it can also be a thing of beauty," He says, making the fire twirl and loop around in his hand. "It looks better at night, though, the dark gives it a magical glow."

"Can you show me how?"

"Yeah, it's simple, just like making a fireball, except you have to concentrate on making it constant, making it stay and move. You need to learn to control it. If you remind me later, when it's dark out, I'll show you just how beautiful it can be."

"Okay," I say.

For the rest of the day we train and practice. We take breaks to eat, drink and talk, and sometimes we just sit in silence, thinking about what's to come.

When it becomes dark, we grab some fallen logs and set them up in a circle. In the middle we place a fire pit; Seth lets me set it.

Everyone sits down on the logs around the fire. I sit beside Seth on one of the logs. Elaina and Keith are sitting on a log together on our left, holding each other close, and Maria and Lucas, who seem to be getting along quite nicely, sit on the log across from us.

"You said you would show me how beautiful fire can be when it gets dark," I whisper to Seth.

"Oh, yeah," Seth says. He extends his arm out in front of him towards the fire, and the fire starts to move. Seth makes it twirl and loop. He makes it go higher and higher into the starlit sky.

This grabs the attention of everyone around the fire. Everyone is staring with awe except for Lucas, who seems uneasy and uncomfortable being so close to fire, which is understandable since he wields Water, its opposite. Lucas inches farther back on his log but, to my admiration, does not leave.

Seth continues to move the fire around. Then he starts making shapes out of it. First he makes a bird that leaves the rest of the fire and flies around us for a while until it disappears. Then he makes a deer, prancing in the fire. Next is a bear, then a fox, then a rabbit. He continues to make shapes. A horse, a goat, even mystical creatures like unicorns and fairies. Then the shape of a human head starts to materialize. Its features turn and shape, the shades of yellow from the fire and black from the night making the shading of the features until it is recognizable. The face is mine. He made my face in the fire. He made me look beautiful and mysterious. He made me look magical.

I turn to look at him and see him staring at me with such gentle yet haunted eyes. Forgetting the audience we have before us, I lean closer, yearning for his kiss. I see conflict in his eyes between what I know he feels for me and the fear of getting hurt if he lets himself admit to his feelings, give in to them. Unfortunately for me the fear of being vulnerable wins, and he pulls away.

He looks at Elaina, Keith, Lucas and Maria. When his gaze rests on me, he whispers, "I'm sorry." Then he gets up and walks into the forest.

We sit there in silence for a moment. Now that Seth is gone, the image of me in the fire has disappeared.

"You should go talk to him," Maria says, breaking the silence.

"Why?" I ask. "He doesn't want me."

"Trust me, he wants you very much. What he doesn't want is the pain he knows he will feel if he were to lose you," Maria explains. "You know as well as I do that he has experienced the pain of the loss of a loved one. And to make things worse, he was locked up for years after, which makes it hard for him to open up, to trust."

I consider what she said for a moment then get up and walk in the direction Seth did, using a little ball of fire to guide me through the dark forest.

CHAPTER 16

I walk for a little while, fireball in hand until I see a little bit of light over by some trees. Assuming it's Seth, I walk towards it.

"Seth?" I say.

"What?" he says with his back towards me.

"Are you all right?"

"Do you feel it too?" he asks, turning to face me.

Taken by surprise, I ask, "Feel what?"

"I don't know how to explain it. The only way I can, it would sound really stupid and cheesy."

"It's okay, you can tell me." I say, excited to hear *him* sound stupid for once.

He hesitates. "A sort of . . . I don't know . . . connection between us. Like a current that runs between us, getting stronger and stronger the more we're together."

I pause, thinking about what he just said. At first I think he's just fooling around, trying to tease me, embarrass me. But when I look into his eyes, I see a vulnerability in him that I've never seen before. I remember thinking almost exactly what he has said about this connection between us getting stronger and stronger the more we're together.

"Um, I'm not really sure what to tell you," I say.

"Just answer my question," he says quietly.

"Yes, I feel it too, but I try to keep it under control because I know it can never be," I say, and I immediately regret it when I see the hurt look on his face.

"Why not?" he asks.

"Because, you don't want it to be. You're too afraid to really care about me," I reply.

"Alright, if that's how you want it."

"Seth," I say.

"What?" he says, his arrogant mask back in place.

"That's not how I want it, and you know it!" I say, raising my voice out of frustration. He flinches at my hostility. "Seth, I'm sorry."

"For what?"

"I don't know," I say, even though what I really want to say is, *I'm sorry for everything that you've been through, and I'm sorry you're too afraid to let me in.*

"I should go now," He says, completely putting what just happened behind him.

"So that's it?" I ask. "You're going to walk away and leave me here, just because you're mad at me?" I am now frustrated with him.

"Yeah, that's pretty much the plan." He starts to go back to the campsite.

I grab his arm and stop him before I even realize what I'm doing. "Don't do this, Seth."

"Don't do what?" he asks clearly wanting nothing more than to get away from me.

"Don't just storm away just because you're mad," I say. "Even though I know you hate it, you need me, you care about me."

"I know I need you. I know I care about you." I am about to say something, but he continues to speak, wanting to get it all out on the table. "I need you to help me defeat this guy. I need you to keep me company. I need you, Rose. Ever since I first saw you, this connection has gotten stronger, and now all I can think about is you—your hair, your eyes, and the way you always have something to say. I hate it, Rose. I hate needing someone, caring about someone."

"Well, sorry for the inconvenience!" I shout.

"Really? That's all you took out of what I just said to you?" Seth shouts back. I take a step back and realize that I've already taken several steps back, and I'm now pinned between him and a tree.

Seth takes another step closer. He looks at me with longing in his eyes. He leans in, closer and closer. Once again my heart beats faster and faster. He puts his arms up on the tree, trapping me in place. I close my eyes, and when our lips finally meet, it's like everything that's happened has disappeared and it's just us. However, as the kiss starts getting deeper and more passionate, he pulls away. "I'm sorry." He says, his lips mere inches from mine.

"For what?" I ask.

"For frustrating you," he says, smirking.

I laugh. "It's okay." I lean in to kiss him again. This time there is this spark, and something pulls us closer together. That connection we were talking about earlier is now so strong, it's as if it is now made of the strongest, most unbreakable fabric. There's no fighting it now, no way to reverse it. Seth puts his arms around my waist, and I put mine around his neck, bringing us closer together.

We return to the campfire where everyone is still sitting. Seth and I sit down on the log we were sitting on before.

"Are you two all right?" Maria asks.

"Yeah," Seth says, putting his arm around my waist and pulling me closer to him.

I nod in agreement. *We are very much all right,* I think to myself.

"Elaina and I are going to go to sleep now," Keith says. They get up and go lie down under the tarp, which is in front of where we sit.

"I'm going to go to bed, too," Maria says, lying down by Elaina and Keith.

"Me too," says Lucas. He joins the others, but to my surprise, he does not lay all that close to Maria.

"You can go to sleep if you want," Seth says.

"What about you?" I ask.

"One of us should keep watch; I'll take the first shift and then wake someone up when I get too tired," he says.

"I'm not tired," I say. "I'll sit with you for a while." I move even closer to Seth and slowly lean my head on his shoulder. He doesn't put his arm around me, but he doesn't move away, either.

"We're probably going to leave the day after tomorrow," he says.

"Are you scared?" I ask.

"Yes."

"Why?"

"Because I finally found you, and I'm not ready to lose you. I haven't even gotten the chance to get used to the idea of us."

"You won't lose me," I say.

Seth stays silent. "You should get some rest," he finally says.

"All right," I say, getting up and lying down next to Lucas.

At first I can't sleep. Seth's words haunt me for some reason. *Why is he sacred? Does he think we'll lose? Why does he think he'll lose me? I'm not even the one fighting this guy.* Finally sleep finds me.

The next day, I wake up to find everyone else is already eating breakfast. "What is this?" I ask, joining the others around the campfire.

"Some berries from the forest," Lucas says.

After we are all done eating, everyone separates into the same pairs as yesterday to train some more.

Seth and I train the same way as yesterday for a little while, and then he decides to show me how to set myself on fire.

First Seth demonstrates. He looks at me slyly and then starts taking off his clothes. "What are you doing?" I shout.

"What do you think happens to our clothes? Do you think they just disappear and reappear?"

"Well, what *do* they do?" I ask, averting my gaze.

"If I kept them on, they would disintegrate into nothing, and then I wouldn't have any clothes at all." He is amused by my refusal to look at him. "You *do* know we're soul mates, right?"

"Yes, but I don't see how that matters. We still barely know each other," I retort, still refusing to look at him.

He laughs. "Well, first of all, you're going to have to look at me if you want to see me turn into fire. Secondly, you're going to have to strip down yourself if you want to try it."

I sigh in defeat and then slowly turn to look at him. As soon as I see his gorgeous, naked body, I can't stop staring. When my eyes meet his, I blush and turn away again. By the smug, arrogant, amused look on his face, he knows I was checking him out.

"How can you just stand there naked like that?" I ask.

"Because it's just you, and I am quite proud of my body and the reaction you had to it," Seth says, barely able to keep himself from laughing. "But seriously, you have to look now. I'm going to do it."

I turn my head and see that he has moved closer to me. He was originally standing over by a tree, a few paces away. Now he is standing a mere arm's length from me. I blush even more, and he obviously sees it because he laughs again.

"Would you just hurry up and set yourself on fire?" I snap.

Seth grins but finally starts explaining how to do it. "First you must find what angers you, and then you must concentrate on feeling heat at your feet." I look down at his feet and see that they are now on fire. "Then you must concentrate on that anger and channel it. Feel the anger become stronger and stronger the more you think about it. Feel it move up you, through you. Harness it, control it, feed off of it." I watch as the flames on his feet rise, consuming his body. Once the flames have covered his whole body, he starts to move around, lift off the ground and change shape.

"Wow," is all I can say as he flies through the air. He lands in front of me and returns to human form. He takes a deep breath, and slowly the flames swirl down his body, leaving Seth in its wake.

"Now you try," he says.

"Put some clothes on first," I demand.

"Why, too distracting for you?" he asks with a smirk.

"Just do it," I say, crossing my arms and rolling my eyes.

He laughs and then goes to put on his clothes.

"Now take yours off," he says, clearly enjoying this.

I squirm uncomfortably but start to take off my clothes, because I know it is the only way I can transform into fire without destroying them completely. I blush and try to cover myself with my arms as best as I can under his gaze as he slowly takes me in. I clear my throat several times before I can get him to focus. When he finally does, we begin.

"Okay, find what makes you angry," he says, still distracted.

I think about my parents.

"Think about setting your feet on fire."

I do.

"Now take the anger and harness it; let it climb all around you, up you, through you. Control it, shape it."

As I do what he says, I can both see and feel the fire consuming me as I slowly become it. When I have completely changed, I fly around and change form. The feeling is magical. I feel so free, no longer stuck on the ground or trapped in the same form. It feels as if I have been doing this forever, it feels so natural, so right. There are no words for it really; wonderful, exquisite, amazing, none of them truly express the greatness of this. I can still see and hear and smell. Everything is the same, except for the fact that I'm on fire, no, I am fire.

I fly around some more. It's fun, and I feel so free. I look down and see Seth has taken off his clothes again and is now changing back into fire. He joins me in the sky, and we fly around each other, kissing, hugging, caressing and laughing until dark.

When it gets dark, we fly around for a little while longer, but only because I refuse to come down because of the glowing beauty of us in the night.

Seth eventually convinces me to come down, reminding me of our big day tomorrow.

Once I'm down, we get dressed and return to the campsite.

"We thought you guys were dead," Lucas jokes.

"You're just in time for dinner," says Elaina. "It's more berries."

Seth and I sit on our log and eat. I tell everyone about turning into fire and that Seth and I are soul mates. The news doesn't seem to surprise Elaina or Maria.

"Remember that favour you promised me?" Seth asks suddenly.

"Yeah, sure," I reply, not fully paying attention. I'm too busy fantasizing about what our life will be like after all of this is over.

"I think I'll be needing it soon," Seth says.

"Okay," I say, confused.

"Tell me you still promise."

I roll my eyes but say it anyways. "I still promise."

After everyone is done eating, Seth, Maria, Keith, Elaina and I go to sleep in the hut. Lucas stays by the fire to take the first watch.

I lay down on my side, and Seth lays down behind me with his arm around me.

CHAPTER 17

The next morning I wake up to find Seth and I are in the same position as when we first went to sleep; it is as if we didn't move at all last night. "Good morning," Seth whispers in my ear.

I smile. "Good morning."

We get up, eat and prepare ourselves as best we can for what is to come; then we head to the boats. Lucas and Keith put the boats into the water, and Seth and I climb into one with Lucas; Maria, Keith and Elaina climb into the other. Seth starts our engine, and both boats start racing off towards the Fire Populous' island.

Once we get there, we quietly make our way through the trees to the King's house. We crouch down at the edge of the woods. Seth hands me the Cinquedea des Morts. "Hide this under your shirt," he says.

"Why?" I ask. "You take it."

"Just hold onto it for me, please?"

"All right," I say, putting the dagger under my waistband and pulling my shirt over it.

"We're going to start here," Seth says. "It's the only place the man would be if he's on the island."

"Why?" I ask.

"Because he has to stay hidden and protected. Now, I'm assuming they've added more security to the place, so we'll have to keep our eyes peeled for guards. If you see one and they see you, kill them as quickly and quietly as possible." Seth pulls out a piece of paper. "This is roughly the layout of the place. There are two floors. Elaina, Lucas and Rose, you'll search the first floor. Keith, Maria and I will take the second floor." Seth pauses and pulls out the picture of Luther. "If you find this man, you must call for the rest of us, and try to keep him from getting away. Take out as many guards as possible."

We start by luring the two guards at the door towards the forest, this time using Maria as bait. We kill the guards and enter the house. At first glance the coast is clear, so Keith, Maria and Seth go upstairs to search and Lucas, Elaina and I start searching the first floor.

Right when we turn a corner, there is a room with glass windows. We immediately go back and out of sight of the four guards guarding the front entrance. We don't kill them because they had their backs turned to us and did not see us. Luther is nowhere to be found.

Just as we are going up the stairs, Keith, Maria and Seth come down, shaking their heads; he's not here. We quickly leave the island and make our way to the Air Populous' island.

"That was fast," I say.

"Yeah, because there weren't many guards, since he wasn't there. If he's at the Air Populous' island, there will be more guards," Seth says.

We arrive at the Air Populous' island with plenty of daylight left. We hide our boats in the bushes by Maria's house, and Maria leads us towards the Air Populous' castle—that's the only word that would describe the way it looks. Whereas the Fire Populous King's house looks like a regular Fire Populous house, no bigger than the others, the Air Populous' castle where the King or Queen lives is huge like a real medieval castle.

"We'd better hurry; there's a lot of ground to cover, and we'll have to stick together here because it's so big. We won't be able to hear each other if someone finds the guy," Seth whispers.

"How do we get in?" I ask. "There are guards everywhere."

"I don't know. I guess we'll have to fight our way in," Seth says.

"On the bright side, because of all of these guards, I think it's safe to assume that he's here somewhere," Lucas says.

Seth turns to face me. "Remember that I love you," he says.

"I love you, too, but this isn't a good-bye type of 'I love you,' right?" I say.

Seth turns without answering. I am about to ask him why he thinks this could be good-bye when he starts moving towards the castle and motions for us to follow. I decide we can discuss it later, because there *will* be a later.

We barely make it to the door before the guards are attacking. They throw wind at us, making it nearly impossible to see, move or even breathe. I look beside me and see Maria is barley affected by this; it does slow her down, but not nearly as much as the rest of us.

Seth starts throwing fireballs in the direction of the castle, but he is unable to really aim due to the wind. "It's no use!" I yell over the roar of the wind. "I think we're actually farther from the door than before!"

Just as I start to give up and let the fierce wind push me back into the forest, the wind stops. I look up and see a giant wall of earth blocking the wind from us. I look back at Elaina and Keith and smile. We stand behind the wall while Elaina and Keith make more of them, in a diagonal line. We slowly move forward, making sure to stay behind the walls of earth. Once we reach the last wall, the rest return to the earth. "We can't get any closer without the ones on the castle balconies being able to get the air over the walls," Elaina says.

"Then we'll have to take them down," Maria says. She moves to the edge of the wall and sticks her head out. Then she puts her arm out, and I hear a giant gust of wind and a bunch of people falling to the ground.

"Come on!" Seth says, and we all leave the safety of the wall to attack the now fallen Air Populous.

Once we get past the first wave of guards, there is no time to lose. We quickly run into the castle by taking out the door completely, and we begin searching for Luther.

We search room after room, floor after floor, tower after tower, taking out the guards we meet on the way. Finally we arrive at the last possible place Luther could be hiding in the castle. We open the door of the last tower to find him there, waiting with an army of Air Populous.

Another battle begins, but there is no earth for Keith or Elaina to use to protect us from the wind, and Maria is too outnumbered. We all try our best by throwing all we have at them, but we cannot do it. In mere minutes they have us captured and bring us to the dungeon.

We are kept there for two days, with the Air Populous only coming down to feed us and give us water. During those long days and the long night I pace around, always looking for a way out, always trying to come up with a plan.

"How can you guys be so calm?" I ask, looking at them lying down or sitting on the floor or on the little beds attached to the wall.

"There's no way out," Seth says.

"How do you know?" I counter.

"Rose, even if there was a way out, the Air Populous guards would catch us right away."

"You don't know that," I say, refusing to give up hope. All of the Populous and humans need us to succeed, after all.

"Yes, I do. We are greatly outnumbered," Seth says.

"He's right," Maria says. "We don't stand a chance against a whole army of Air Populous."

"Why aren't they killing us?" I ask.

"I don't know," Maria answers.

"This makes no sense. He has us, so why doesn't he kill us. Once we're dead, there will be nothing to stop him," I say.

I hear footsteps descending the stairs. *It must be the Air Populous bringing us our dinner,* I think to myself.

When the footsteps stop, I look up and see Luther, my parents and some guards. I gasp in surprise. I was not expecting my parents here.

I get up from where I was sitting beside Seth in the dungeon. Keith, Elaina, Lucas, Maria and Seth all get up, too. "What do you want?" I ask rudely.

"Well, they want to kill you," my father says, motioning to Luther and the Air Populous guards. "And frankly, after all you've done, I wouldn't really care, but your mother insisted that we give you a chance to live."

I look over at Luther, who is smiling deviously. My father continues. "I'm sure you've already figured out about the spell Seth's parents cast on you all those years ago."

"Yes, we have," I say.

"The one where you can only kill one without killing the otherif one of you kills the other."

"Yes, we know but what does it have to do with—wait, you're saying if I kill Seth, you'll let me live?" I ask, bewildered that they would even suggest that, although they probably don't know that he's my soul mate and that I'm in love with him.

"That is exactly what I am saying," Father says.

"No way. I'd rather die," I say, crossing my arms and looking away defiantly.

"She'll do it," Seth says.

I turn and look at him in shock. "What!?" I exclaim.

"Very well, we will return in 10 minutes. You may all say your good-byes. Oh, I almost forgot: Rose is the only one who will survive. The rest of you will be executed shortly after Seth," Father says, leaving with Mother, Luther and the Air Populous guards following closely behind.

I continue to stare at Seth, speechless. I finally find my voice and say, "I don't know what's going on in your crazy head, but there is absolutely no way I will kill you," I say.

Seth looks at me calmly. "Remember that favour you promised me?"

"Yeah . . ."

"Well, I'm calling it in."

"What? No way!" I scream. "I won't do it! You can't make me!"

"You promised me I could ask you to do anything, and you would do it," Seth says, still calm.

"How can you ask me to do this? I thought you loved me!" I say as I go from stunned to angry to devastated in seconds.

"Rose," he says gently, taking my hand in his. "It's okay, I've prepared myself for this. I'll be okay."

"What do you mean, you've prepared yourself for this?" I ask, barely able to get those words out as I try to hold on to my sanity.

Seth takes my other hand, which was fisted so tight my knuckles are white, and there is golden-yellow blood flowing from the little cuts my fingernails have made in my palm. He gently makes me loosen my fist until he holds it flat in his other hand. He takes a deep breath and then says, "It was never me who was supposed to take on this man. From the beginning I decided that you would be the one to do it, and you can't do it otherwise."

"Why?" I ask.

"Because if you're dead, you won't be able to do it." Seth says, trying to lighten the mood—which is stupid, because this mood is not about to become any lighter.

"You know what I mean," I say. "Why do I have to do it? Why can't you?"

"Because to kill this man, the person who wields fire, his original element, has to be very strong. To be as strong as you need to be, you have to absorb my power over fire from me by reciting the words, 'I have taken your life; I will now take your power' once I'm dead. You will then have enough power to finish him off. You'll be able to kill him and save the Populous and the humans."

"I still don't see why you can't!" I protest.

"Because I'm not killing you, and you owe me a favour. You promised."

"That's not fair, and you know it!" I sob.

"Life isn't fair, Rose."

"I won't do it."

"You will, and when I'm dead, you have to remember to kill him. The others already know what to do. But remember, you have to hit him last. You have to be the one to do it."

"Wait, they *knew* this would happen? They knew all along?" I yell. "Did you plan this whole thing from the very beginning? This whole time you were just following your stupid plan? You were banking on them catching us, weren't you? You knew the whole time they would, because that's what you planned to happen! All of that time spent training, that wasn't for you guys, was it? It was so that *I* could train! So I would know how to use my powers! So what? Did your plan go something like this: Get Rose to fall for you, get captured by the enemy and get Rose to kill you so she'll absorb your power and be strong enough to kill Luther. Then what's next? Nothing! Nothing is next, because you'd be dead. Well, guess what! There's one thing you didn't count on: me refusing to kill you. You made me fall in love with you, and no matter how well-thought-out your little plan was, you didn't think about what would happen if I refused to do it, did you?" I pause for a moment to catch my breath. "Wait, why did you make me fall in love with you? Are you sure you really love me?"

"Because in the beginning, *I* was going to kill *you* and absorb your power, so I could be the one who killed Luther! I figured if you were in love with me, it would be easier to get you to sacrifice yourself. What I didn't count on was falling in love with you and wanting to sacrifice myself instead," Seth says.

"You were going to kill me and take my power?" I ask, startled by what he just said. I had never even considered that possibility.

"Yes, I was."

"But, you fell in love with me, and you don't want to kill me anymore?"

"Yes."

I ponder his words for a moment. Should I feel angry? Betrayed? Sad? I don't feel any of those emotions. Right now none of that matters. What matters is that he now wants me to kill him. I look over at Keith, Elaina, Maria and Lucas and remember one of my earlier questions. "They knew?" I ask again.

"Yes. I told them, Rose! They had to know so that they knew what to do after I was dead!" Seth begins. "And yes, I planned this whole thing, and everything is going as planned. Soon Luther will be dead, and everyone will be free." Seth rushes on before I can interrupt and remind him that if he were to have it his way, he'd be dead, too. "And at first getting you to fall in love with me was nothing but part of my plan, but then it became so much more than that, Rose." He strokes my cheek. "Then it became real and fun and wonderful. So the answer to your last question is that I do really love you—there is no way I couldn't, because we're soul mates, remember?"

"Yes, I remember," I whisper closing my eyes as he pulls me into his arms.

"And you can't fake being soul mates. It's not possible."

"I know, but I still I refuse to do it," I say.

Seth doesn't say anything.

A few minutes later, Air Populous guards come to get us. They bring us outside into a courtyard, and there are guards everywhere. There is no escape. They push us into the middle of a circle of guards. My parents and Luther stand front and center, waiting for me to kill Seth. *Well, joke's on them*, I think to myself. *I'm not going to kill Seth.*

I look over to the side and see what I assume is the Air Populous Queen. She wears a gray halter dress and has white, glowing tattoo designs all over her body. She looks on with a blank look on her face.

I stand there and stare at them. Luther throws a knife by my feet. I continue to stand there and stare them down.

All of a sudden Seth grabs the knife and puts it in my hands. When I try to drop it, he grips my hands in between his and won't let me. I start to panic. I scream and yell and try to pull away from him, but it's no use—he's stronger than me and is just as determined to have me kill him as I am to *not* do it.

As the knife draws closer and closer to his stomach, I start to go crazy and fight against him with all I have. I see the knife pierce his stomach, once, twice. Seth lets go of the knife and falls to the ground. I fall to my knees beside him. *He's still alive! I can save him!* I tell myself. I try to stop the bleeding, but the blood continues to flow.

Seth grabs my hands in his. I look at him, pleading for him to stay with me. "Remember," he says, only to choke on his blood, which is now flowing out of his mouth. He clears his throat as best he can and continues in a hoarse, barely audible voice. "Remember to kill him," he says. "And remember that I love you." Then he dies. Just like that, he is dead. One moment he's convulsing from the pain and shock, and the next he's completely still, with vacant eyes staring up at me. I close his eyes and stand up. I recite the words he told me to say earlier and feel his power flowing into me. It feels like breathing in fresh air after suffocating, drinking the freshest water after nearly dying from dehydration, eating the most delicious meal after not eating for days. It feels invigorating, refreshing and wonderful. I look over at Seth's body and can see a string of yellow fog flowing out of his body and into mine. Once the flow of power stops, I turn to face my enemies.

I glare at them, full of rage, despair and sadness. I'm almost overwhelmed by these feelings. The only thing keeping me from collapsing back down and sobbing is the determination I have to kill this man—for Seth, for the Populous', for the humans and for me. I take one step forward, my gaze settling on Luther. I am about to kill him when I remember that I am supposed to be the last to hit him. I turn to face Keith, Elaina, Lucas and Maria. "Now!" I yell.

Immediately, Elaina and Keith create a dome around us and Luther with the earth; each pulls up half of it using quick hand motions. Now my parents and the Air Populous cannot interfere. Maria uses her power over air to knock his air ability right out of him. Then Lucas knocks his water power out of him, taking away that power as well. Next Keith knocks the power of earth out of him, leaving him with only fire.

Finally it is my turn. I channel all of my rage and focus on one thing; to kill the man who has caused so much pain. Not just my pain, but the pain of so many others. With just one blow he will be human, with no power over any of the elements. Then I will kill him with the Cinquedea des Morts and in doing so free the spirits of the Populous he killed in order to be able to wield all of the elements. I'll free the Populous and humans from a terrible fate. I stare him down and hold my hand out, pointing it in his direction. The Populous on the other side of the wall are slowly breaking it down, piece by piece. I have to hurry before all our work and sacrifice becomes for nothing.

All of my anger and pain flows straight from my heart and out through my hand. I feel pure satisfaction when I see the scared look on Luther's face as the giant ball of fire flies towards him. Once it makes contact, he flies back and hits the wall of earth Elaina and Keith created. His power over fire is now gone; he is a mere human. I walk over to his helpless body and quickly slit his throat, taking his life from him the way he took everything from me. Because of him I lost my home, my parents and Seth. Now we are somewhat even.

Elaina and Keith slowly take down what remains of the wall of earth, and I brace myself for an attack. When none comes, I take a close look at the people outside. They all stare at us, confused. *They don't remember—The spell is broken!*

I look to Maria, Elaina, Keith and Lucas, and they all smile at me. I smile back. *We did it!* But my glory is short-lived. I drop down beside Seth and sit there, holding his limp hand and crying. I wipe my eyes and look at my hand with wonder. Instead of water leaking down my cheeks, this warm, pale yellow liquid flows down. I don't cry often—in fact I can't remember the last time I cried, and I certainly don't remember what it looked like. I continue to sit there and cry, making no move to get up. The only movement I make is shaking, not from the cold but from pure sadness and despair. My adventure, my everything is now gone, dead. *Elaina, Keith, Lucas and Maria can take care of everything else,* I think to myself. *Right now it takes everything I have not to snap, to break.*

I am left alone until it gets dark out. Maria comes out and sits down beside me. She starts gently rubbing slow, calming circles on my back. I have stopped crying, but only barely. It's like a huge part of me is dead.

"Keith and Elaina left to go see how things are doing on the Earth Populous' island, to see if everyone is free of the man's spell now that he is dead. They said they would check on the Fire Populous' island as well. Lucas went to see how the Water Populous is doing, and the Air Populous are fine. Your parents are a little worse than the others, probably because they were so close to him. They may need more time to recover."

I say nothing, but the news does make me feel a little bit better. At least I'll have my parents back, although things will never be the same with them. I'll always remember what they did while under the spell.

Maria sits with me for a little while as I continue to kneel beside his body. "I've heard that some people die from the hurt of losing their soul mate," she says.

"I wish I had," I say. "I finally had him, and we never got to have a normal relationship. We were always doing something that would lead to the death of Luther. We never even had an official first date." I feel the tears returning to my eyes.

"We should probably let the guards take his body now," Maria says.

"No!" I say, putting myself between them.

"Rose, it can't stay here forever. *You* can't stay here forever."

"Can you hear him?" I ask.

Maria pauses. "No, not yet," she says, to my despair.

"If you ever hear him, you'll tell me, right?" I ask.

"Yes, but Rose, you have to remember he's dead. You can't have a relationship with him through me. You're going to have to try to move on."

"I *can't* move on, I'll never move on—I'm the one who killed him!"

"You didn't want to. He made you, Rose. Seth dying wasn't your fault. It was Luther's."

Seth is all I can think about. Our time shared together flashes through my mind over and over, from when I first let him out of that room till now. I think about our fights, the fun we had together, our first kiss. I've been continuously running through the memories, remembering him, remembering more details every time. His smirk, his arrogant tone, the times he let me in and opened up to me, his gentleness . . . his love. I try to find hints of his plan. I try to find ways I could have known what he was planning to do this whole time, if I had only paid more attention. He gave me everything, and in return I took everything. He gave me my adventure, he gave me his love; he saved my life more than once. And the one time he needed me to save his, I couldn't even do that.

"Rose, he's not coming back. He can't be brought back from the dead."

Maria's words echo in my head. *He can't be brought back from the dead.* My time with Seth runs through my memory again, this time focusing on a conversation we had had. *"Well,"* he had said, *"we know for sure that there are Populous for all four of the elements: fire, water, earth and air. But some people say there are Populous for the element of Spirit. It is said that they used to be the primary peacekeepers for all of the elements. Apparently they were very powerful. They could do what we could only dream of doing: they could bring spirits back from the dead. If a loved one died and you were able to find their island and bring the body to them, they could heal the body and bring the spirit back to it. Legend has it that they are still out there somewhere; they just hid themselves because so many people came to them, wanting their loved ones brought back from the dead. Knowing this was wrong, the Spirit Populous hid themselves, never to be seen again."*

"Get the guards to wrap up his body, but gently so that it can be undone," I say with new hope rising inside of me.

"Why?" Maria asks suspiciously.

"Um, it's a human thing," I lie.

"All right," Maria says, getting up to get the guards.

A few moments later, they are taking Seth's body and wrapping it up in cloth. "Now put it in one of the boats," I order.

"Rose, what do you plan on doing?" she asks.

"It's a send-off," I say.

She looks suspicious but motions for the guards to do as I say.

Once the body is in one of the motor boats we used to get here, I quickly jump in and start it, speeding away. I hear Maria calling after me but ignore her. Instead I make the boat go faster until it is far enough out so that the Air Populous have no way of bringing me back.

The island gets smaller and smaller until I can no longer see it. It is dark out, so I can barely see where I am going, but it doesn't really matter because I have no idea where I am going.

All of a sudden the motor makes funny noises, and the boat slows down until it stops altogether. Great, it's out of fuel. I grab the oars that are in the boat and start rowing. I row and row, never stopping, never slowing. I have only one destination, and I will not stop until I reach it. I will not stop rowing until I reach the Spirit Populous' island.

I look at Seth's body, now wrapped up, and I pull out the rose he gave me a few nights earlier. It feels like forever ago. I twirl it around between my fingers a few times and stare at it. Every time I changed clothes, I made sure I placed it carefully under my waistband. It's a little beat up but still beautiful all the same. I gently place the rose on his chest, and then I whisper to him, "I have a new promise for you." I close my eyes and hope that somehow he can hear me. "Hang in there, Seth, because I promise to bring you back."

CPSIA information can be obtained at www.ICGtesting.com
Printed in the USA
LVOW130827170113

316010LV00003B/17/P